Pan's Secret: A Pirate Princess's Quest for Answers

The Pirate Princess Chronicles, Volume 2

R.V. Bowman

Published by R.V. Bowman, 2019.

PAN'S SECRET: A PIRATE PRINCESS'S QUEST FOR ANSWERS

First edition. May 10, 2019.

Written by R.V. Bowman.

In Dedication to my Mother,

Mary Ann McColm

Thanks for always being willing to read

just one more story.

Chapter 1:
Everything is Wonderful...Or Not

The sun was barely a glow on the horizon when the boat hit the water, and Smee began rowing toward the shore. Andromeda Cavendish looked across at her father in the dim pre-morning light. She still couldn't quite believe that she was here. That after years of wishing and dreaming about it, she would actually be spending the entire summer with him. Of course, that wish hadn't come true exactly the way she imagined it would. Until a few days ago, she had no idea James Cavendish led a secret life, that he was a pirate named Captain Hook on a magical island. Rommy had thought her father headed up a prosperous shipping company, spending his time traveling the seas, and that was why he visited her so rarely. The truth took a bit of getting used to.

She let out a little sigh.

Hearing her, Hook caught her eye and smiled. "Are you re-thinking our early start, Rommy?" he asked. "I'm afraid showing up this early, we might catch Chief Hawk Eye and his people still in their beds," he said.

"Oh no, Papa," she said, leaning toward him. "I really don't think we can wait. After yesterday, there's no telling what Pan will try."

Before Hook could answer, Smee gave his own sigh as he pulled on the oars. "I don't know what you were thinking, leaving this early," he said and sniffed. "Hardly ate your breakfast, either of you, and Rommy, poor lamb, injured, and you as well, Captain. If you ask me, neither of you is in any shape to be going anywhere."

Her father glowered at Smee. "I don't recall asking you anything, Smee," he said. He gestured with his hook toward the shore that wasn't far off now. "If you know what's good for you, I suggest you keep your opinions to yourself and row."

The small man's face turned red. He tried to salute but almost hit himself in the head with the oar he was holding. He swallowed and bobbed his head up and down instead. "Just as you say, Captain, just as you say."

Turning to Rommy, Hook patted her knee and winced. He had refused the sling Smee had made for him, but he kept the arm Peter Pan had slashed against his body. Rommy didn't know how he had managed to put on his red leather coat. For that matter, she wasn't sure how Smee had found time to repair the tear from Pan's dirk. He had even managed to find her another set of clean clothes and hot water to take a bath last night.

As the shore got closer, Rommy chewed her bottom lip. Her father wasn't well liked in Neverland. "Papa," she began, choosing her words carefully, "when we get there, maybe I should talk to Chief Hawk Eye about Alice. He seems very honorable, and I know he'll let her go with me, but I'm not sure..." she trailed off.

Hook raised an eyebrow. "Are you worried that Chief Hawk Eye won't want to entrust Alice to someone like me, Rommy?"

Rommy's face flushed, and she stared down at her hands. "Well, Papa, he does think you were going to let Tiger Lily drown just to find out where Pan's hideout was." She raised her eyes and, to her surprise, saw a twinkle in her father's.

"My dear, have a little faith in your old Papa," he said. The side of his mouth kicked up. "After all, Chief Hawk Eye sent you off with Pan and you almost drowned, too. I'd say the Chief is a fair enough man to call us even, don't you?"

Rommy shrugged, but a smile tugged at her mouth. The teasing, smiling man in front of her was more like the Papa she remembered from what she now thought of as pre-Neverland. Since arriving on the magical island, she'd seen a side of her father that had surprised her, and if she was very honest, rather horrified her, too.

The boat bumped into the shore, but before she could clamber out, her father had swung her onto the rock-strewn sand. Rommy wished she could fly, but since Hook couldn't, she fell into step with him. She had to take three steps for every one of his as he strode forward.

By the time they drew within sight of the Indian encampment, the sun had risen in the sky. Rommy could see smoke rising from the fire pit in the center of the circle of tents. She recognized Little Owl who was tending something in a pot. She gripped her father's arm, and he stopped just outside a cluster of large rocks.

Seeing her chewing her lip, he patted her hand. "Don't worry, my dear. Chief Hawk Eye is an honorable man," he said. "We'll have Alice and be headed back before you know it."

He smiled at her, and despite her worries, she smiled back. She turned back toward the encampment, ready to get Alice.

A scuffle behind one tent caught her attention, and Rommy squinted to get a better view. When she realized who it was, her blood chilled.

Chapter 2:
Tiger Lily's Plan

Rommy had almost missed Tiger Lily and her small hostage as they slipped out the back of one of the tall, conical dwellings. Even trussed up like a Christmas goose, though, Alice was not making it easy on her captor. It was Alice's struggle that had caught her eye. The six-year-old girl, despite her tiny size, was fighting the older girl every step of the way. For each foot of progress Tiger Lily made, Alice retreated half the distance.

Rommy grabbed at her father's arm and pointed at the two girls. Tiger Lily struggled to pull the resisting Alice away from the other dwellings before anyone heard them.

Even from here, Rommy could see the anger in the older girl's posture. Tiger Lily leaned close to Alice, and the early morning light glinted off an object Tiger Lily held in her hand. She waved the knife in Alice's face.

"Papa," Rommy said, her voice low, "we have to stop her. She's probably taking Alice to Pan. We can't let him have her. There's no telling what he'll do, especially after yesterday."

Scenes from her sword fight with Peter Pan flashed through her mind. She shuddered as she recalled the look in his cold, brown eyes when he promised she'd pay. Fear formed

5

a lead ball in her stomach when she realized the person who might end up paying was Alice. They had to stop Tiger Lily.

Rommy moved forward to sound the alarm, but Hook stopped her. "Wait a moment, my dear," he said.

She looked at him in surprise. Hook's eyes narrowed as he stared at Tiger Lily and Alice. Rommy felt a dart of unease.

"We can't wait, Papa," said Rommy. "We have to stop her before she gets too far from the encampment. Chief Hawk Eye doesn't know about this. I know he'll be more likely to give Alice over to us if he sees she isn't safe with him and Little Owl."

"Don't fear, Daughter," said Hook, a smile curving his lips. "We won't let Alice slip through our fingers, but we might just catch a bigger prize along with her." He gestured with his hook. "Be as silent as you can."

"What are you talking about? We need to raise the alarm, not be silent," Rommy said.

"Andromeda...Rommy, has it not occurred to you that young Tiger Lily can lead us straight to Pan? He certainly won't be expecting me this morning when he meets up with his young, lovelorn friend here."

"But Papa, what about Alice? Won't that put her in terrible danger?" Rommy frowned. She wanted to trust Papa, but the sinking feeling in her stomach told her differently.

"Nonsense, my dear," said Hook. "We'll have the upper hand if we can follow the girl without her realizing it. Pan will never know what hit him, and we'll have Alice back on the ship before you know it."

Rommy bit her lip, but she knew they needed to do something soon or risk Tiger Lily slipping away with Alice. Papa was right. If they did follow Tiger Lily, they needed the element of surprise on their side.

Observing her indecision, Hook pressed his advantage. "If I can get Pan, I don't have to stay here. Don't you see? We can go back to England. Together."

Rommy's heart gave a pang. If she was honest, she didn't just want the summer with Papa. She wanted a real life with him. In England.

Hook held out more incentive. "With Pan out of the way, there's no reason you can't return to Chattingham's. I'm sure you miss Francie and your other little friends."

The minutes slipped by, but still Rommy hesitated. Her unease didn't lessen, but if Papa could get Pan...Finally, she nodded. "Okay, but Alice needs to be our first priority—even if that means Pan gets away."

"Of course," said Hook. He gripped her shoulder and then winced. Another stab of doubt rippled through Rommy.

"Are you sure you can fight, Papa? You're injured, and my arm is still sore. Maybe we shouldn't chance it."

Hook frowned, but he kept his voice even. "I told you, we'll have the element of surprise. He won't get away this time." His eyes narrowed again and zeroed in on Tiger Lily. His jaw clenched so tightly, Rommy could hear his teeth grinding.

"Papa?" Rommy touched his arm, and he startled, as if he had forgotten she was there. "Shouldn't we follow them, before Tiger Lily gets too far away?"

"Patience, my dear," said Hook, his smile returning. "Learn from your papa. We'll just give her a bit more room. There isn't a lot of cover here where we can stay hidden. We'll have to rely

on silence and the long grasses by the river to help us. It won't
do us any good if the Chief or one of his people sees us, either."

"But what about..." Rommy started, but Hook cut her off.

"Let's go. Remember, silently." He glided out from behind
the rocks and motioned her to follow him.

Rommy could see Tiger Lily moving through the swaying
grasses that covered this part of the island, her progress uneven
and choppy. Behind her, a small, dark head bobbed up and
down. She smiled. Alice was still fighting Tiger Lily every step
of the way.

Her smile fell away as she looked at the gently waving sea
of vegetation that stretched out, the grass getting thicker the
closer it got to the riverbank. She hoped those swaying fronds
hid nothing else. Rommy shuddered as she remembered the
red flower she had seen when she had first arrived in the magical island. It had looked so beautiful—right until it had lunged
up and eaten a bird flying amongst its blooms.

Hook made an impatient sound and gestured toward her
again. Rommy slipped from behind the rock and followed him.
For a big man, he moved silently, crouched low, so he blended
into the grasses.

She followed in his wake. Worry churned in her stomach.
This was a bad idea. She knew it. They should have just stopped
Tiger Lily before she had even left the encampment. It would
have been so easy. Rommy sighed. It was too late now.

Her father's crouched frame moved forward in front of her
and the endless sea of grasses swayed on either side of her. She
strained her eyes into the blades, hoping to see any dangers
lurking there.

After a seeming eternity, her father came to a sudden halt, flattening himself even further into the grass. Rommy stared at him. It was amazing how small he could make himself, she thought, before he grabbed her arm and pulled her down, too.

She sucked in a breath as her injured arm protested. Hook made an apologetic face and pointed ahead. Peeking around him, Rommy saw the willow tree where she and Alice had stopped to rest, only to find themselves captured a few days ago.

Had it only been a few days? She felt a pang when she remembered her best friend Francie and her school. When she had sneaked away from the Chattingham School for Modern Girls looking for her father, she had thought it would only be for a day. Things had taken a decidedly surprising turn since then.

An angry screech brought her back to the present. Tiger Lily stood under the tree, rubbing her shin. Next to her was the smaller form of Alice. Rommy smirked. If they just distracted Tiger Lily long enough, Alice could surely get away.

Although she was only six, Alice had been living on the streets of London when Rommy had met her. She would help in her own rescue if given half a chance. Rommy glanced at her father, wondering what he would think of the little girl. Alice's habit of speaking her mind and her father's formidable temper might make things rather interesting.

Rommy felt her father's body stiffen next to her as a crowing laugh carried on the breeze. Pan was here.

Chapter 3:
Everything Goes Wrong

Rommy's shoulders stiffened, and a knot of cold dread formed in her belly. All her doubts about this ambush swept over her in a rush. Her father hardly had the use of his arm, and she was still hurting where Pan had sliced her in their sword fight. The last thing she wanted was another confrontation.

She gripped her father's arm. "What now?" she mouthed.

He leaned in closer, his voice barely audible in her ear. "I'll wait until Pan is closer. Then I'll ambush him." A cold smile curved Hook's lips. "By the time he realizes I'm there, it will be too late."

"But what about Alice? We have to make sure she's safe," Rommy said. "Do you want me to distract Tiger Lily?"

Hook shook his head. "Absolutely not. You will stay here, out of harm's way. Once I take care of Pan, Tiger Lily won't be an issue."

"But Papa..." Rommy protested, but Hook cut her off.

"That's final, Andromeda," he said. "You will wait here." His gaze didn't leave her face.

Rommy pressed her lips together and looked back at him. Hook's brows came together in a frown. "Don't make me regret bringing you, Andromeda," he said. "Promise me you will stay here."

After another moment, she reluctantly nodded. Now wasn't the time to get in a fight with her father. Hook turned back to watch his prey, and Rommy's hand drifted to the small sheath at her waist that concealed a dagger.

Thinking they were going on a peaceful visit to Chief Hawk Eye, Rommy hadn't brought her sword, but Neverland was full of strange and dangerous things. The dagger had made her feel safer. Now, though, it seemed a meager defense against Pan or even Tiger Lily.

Rommy felt a rustle beside her as her father crept forward. His big frame slid silently through the grass, and she again wondered how he could stay so low and move so silently. He moved several yards toward the tree. She crept behind him, staying close.

Rommy could hear Pan talking, but the wind whipped away his words. She could see Alice leaning away from Pan. Even from this distance, Rommy could see the rigidness in the little girl's body.

"Hang on, Alice," she murmured under her breath. "We're coming."

At that moment, her father exploded out of the grass. Rommy watched as everything seemed to happen at once.

Her father, catching Pan by surprise, had latched onto his shirt with his hook. Her father held his jeweled dagger to Pan's throat, but Rommy could see he was having trouble using his arm.

Alice, using the distraction, had knocked Tiger Lily to her knees. Seeing her opportunity, Alice took off, but with her arms tied to her sides, her balance was off. She tripped and fell. The older girl lunged at her, grabbing Alice's legs. Alice kicked at the older girl and squirmed further out of reach.

Taken up with the scene in front of her, Rommy had floated into the air for a better view without even realizing it. While Hook grappled with Pan, Tiger Lily dragged Alice to her feet. The sun's rays glinted off the knife in Tiger Lily's hand.

Before she knew what she was doing, Rommy had shot toward the other girl, who now had the knife pointed at Alice. As she rushed toward the fight, she caught sight of movement out of the corner of her eye and whipped her head around.

The large crocodile Pan called Old Crocky was heaving itself up on the bank of the river. The grasses parted around it as it slithered forward at a frightening speed. Right toward Pan and her father.

"Papa!" she screamed.

Everything was happening too fast. Her father's snapped his head in her direction, and Pan, using the distraction, wrenched away from him, whipping out his own dirk.

Now her father was trapped between Pan and the crocodile. Tiger Lily had Alice pulled up against her with the knife pointed at the little girl.

"Looks like you're in a pickle, Captain," Pan said. He threw back his head and let out a cackle. Then he spotted Rommy.

"Well, look who's here, our little hero." Pan's lip curled in a sneer. "Always running to the rescue, aren't you, Rommy? But I don't think your sword fighting will get your dear old father out this predicament."

Rommy's eyes darted from Alice to her father to the crocodile, which was still moving at an alarming rate. If she could distract Pan, maybe Papa could get to safety, but that still left Alice at the mercy of Tiger Lily.

Rommy's eyes met Alice's. The little girl was pale behind the gag tied around her mouth, but there was a look of determination on her small face. Alice's eyes cut to Pan, and she tipped her head back toward Tiger Lily who was currently ignoring her to glare at Rommy.

Rommy gave a brief nod and rocketed toward Pan with a loud cry. At that moment, Alice slammed her head back against Tiger Lily's chin and stomped on her foot. The little girl didn't hesitate but pushed into the air out of Tiger Lily's reach.

Rommy knocked into Pan as the crocodile lunged toward her father. Hook leapt toward the tree and scrambled up into its branches. The beast's jaws snapped shut, missing Hook's left foot by mere inches. Tiger Lily, seeing the massive reptile so close, fled in the opposite direction, out of the creature's reach.

The force of Rommy's midair tackle tumbled her and Pan through the air, and his dirk dropped to the ground. She gripped her dagger but hoped she wouldn't have to use it. She was still tired and sore from the battle the previous evening. In a close fight, even with her dagger, she didn't know if she had the strength to best him.

Pan pushed away from her, his teeth bared in a snarl. "You might have saved your worthless father, but you can't save them both." Before she realized what he meant to do, Pan had spun in the air and swooped down on Alice. The little girl, hampered by her bonds, couldn't fly very fast. Pan caught her with ease.

Wrapping the girl in a bear hug, he turned to Rommy. "I don't know why you keep saving him, anyway. He's not worth it!"

Didn't we have this conversation already?" Rommy said. She pushed her chin up, but her dagger trembled. "If you think I'm going to let you take Alice, you *are* a slow learner." She kept her eyes trained on Pan, looking for an opportunity.

"Stay away from him," said Hook. Rommy glanced at her father. He perched in the tree, his face white and tense. He couldn't help her or Alice now. She turned her gaze back to Pan.

"You're the slow learner," he said and jerked his head in Hook's direction. "He doesn't care about you. If he did, he wouldn't be chasing me, now would he? He certainly wouldn't have risked little Alice here." Rommy flinched, and Pan smiled. "He probably promised he'd rescue Alice, didn't he? How many promises has he broken since you got here?"

Rommy gripped her dagger tighter and moved closer. Pan backed away, tightening his hold on Alice, who wiggled and squirmed. "Oh, I don't think so," he said. A smile curved across his face. "Don't follow us—unless you want me to feed her to Old Crocky here." He nodded toward the reptile who was lying on the bank of the river. The creature's large head was swinging back and forth, looking for all the world like it was watching a performance.

Before he turned and sped away, Alice's eyes met Rommy's. The fear in them squeezed her heart.

Chapter 4:
Papa Disappoints

Rommy hovered in the air, feeling numb as she watched Pan and Alice become mere specks in the sky. She blinked rapidly to keep the tears that were welling in her eyes from falling.

Her father was sitting on a tree branch, keeping a wary eye on the crocodile that was still lying on the bank. Although it was motionless, its yellow eyes tracked Hook's every move. It would have been funny, seeing her father perched in a tree, if Alice were here. But she wasn't.

Pan's words played over in her mind, and the fog of numbness burned away as anger flared. Rommy buzzed down to hover in front of her father.

"How could you?" she asked in a choked voice. "I told you we should have stopped Tiger Lily before she even left the encampment, but no, you had to go after Pan. And now Alice is gone." Her voice caught on the last word, and she clenched her jaw to keep from crying. "She's gone, and we don't even know where Pan took her!"

Hook held out his hand to her. "Now, Andromeda...Rommy, you don't understand. I had to try, and I was so close this time." He glanced down at the crocodile, irritation crossing his face. "If it hadn't been for that ridiculous beast, we'd all be on our way home together right now."

"But we're not all on our way home, are we?" Rommy retorted. "You're stuck up in a tree. Pan took Alice who knows where, and you could have died." Rommy took a deep breath, trying to regain her composure. "I don't know why you want Pan so badly, but he's not worth all this! He's not worth Alice!" Rommy dashed a hand across her face as tears leaked out despite her best efforts.

Hook's face contorted. "I'm sorry, Rommy, but you don't understand."

"You're right, Papa," said Rommy, her lips thinning to a hard line. "I don't understand. I really don't."

Turning away from her father, she started to fly away.

"Rommy, wait!" he said, but she kept going. "Andromeda Cavendish, you come back here right now. Don't you fly away from me."

She whirled back to face him, unable to contain the hurt and anger churning inside. "Why? So you can make another promise you'll only end up breaking? Pan was right about that, wasn't he?" Rommy gave a bitter laugh.

"You don't understand, Rommy," Hook said again.

"Then why won't you help me understand?" said Rommy, staring into her father's eyes. Hook was the first to look away.

He opened his mouth to speak, but Rommy was done. She spun away from him and, putting on a burst of speed, headed toward the ship, unsure where else to go. The tears she had been trying to keep back fell thick and fast down her cheeks, the wind blowing them back into her hair.

Thoughts of Alice crowded out her disappointment in her father. The little girl wasn't afraid of much. When Rommy met her, Alice had been facing down a gang of bullies three times her size, but Pan terrified her. And Rommy didn't blame her. Pan looked like a boy about her own age, but when you looked into his eyes, he was ancient. Ancient and scary.

Rommy felt her anger flare again. She didn't know what had brought Papa to Neverland or what drove him to exact revenge on Pan, but she felt her dreams of their spending time together crash down around her. She had thought they could get to know each other. Deep down, what she really hoped was that they could leave Neverland, go back to England. Be a family.

With a sinking heart, Rommy realized that her father's desire for revenge overshadowed everything, even her and definitely Alice. And she wasn't sure she could forgive him for that.

Chapter 5:
Now What?

Before Rommy even touched down on the ship, Smee was hurrying over to her. His eyes were wide with worry, and he was wringing his hands.

"My dear girl, whatever is wrong?" he asked. He grasped her arms and looked her over. "Are you hurt? Where's the Captain? Don't tell me something's happened to him."

Rommy swiped at the tears that refused to stop. "No, I'm not hurt, and Papa's fine. Well, he's stuck up a tree, but he's otherwise fine." Rommy stopped and gulped. "But...but...Pan took Alice." Her voice broke, and the tears fell faster.

Smee stared at her. He opened and closed his mouth several times before he spoke. "Up a tree? Pan?"

By this time, several of the other pirates were gathered around Rommy and Smee; they peppered her with questions.

"What's happened, lass?" asked Big Red, a giant of a man with a flaming beard that fell to his waist. "Are ye hurt?"

"A tree, ye say? Wot's he doin' up there?" Stubbs asked. His good eye squinted in confusion.

"Were the Indians in league with Pan? Who's Alice? Don't tell me the Captain has another daughter!" Tommy, the cabin boy, smacked his forehead at the idea.

Rommy put her hands out, trying to ward off the questions flying at her so fast they made her head spin.

An arm came around her shoulders and a somewhat rumpled handkerchief appeared in front of her face. "Patience, lads," a smooth voice said. "The poor girl can't answer you all at once. She's obviously had an upset. Let's give her a moment to compose herself, and then I'm sure the young lady will share what happened with all of us."

"Aw, why don't ya speak plain, Gentleman Jack?" called Stubbs.

"Stop smothering the girl, so she can answer your questions," the man called Gentleman Jack said. "Is that plain enough for you, Stubbs?"

Rommy mopped at her eyes with the handkerchief.

"Thank you, sir," she said, trying to hand back his handkerchief. He folded her hand over it and squeezed.

"Don't you worry about it," he said with a wink. He had a head full of wavy dark hair and twinkling golden-brown eyes. Unlike most of the men, his clothes looked dashing rather than dirty.

Speaking of the men, they were all staring at her, waiting for her to speak. Rommy's cheeks burned. Last night they were cheering her win over Pan. Now, she was blotchy and tear-stained. She cleared her throat and tried to gather her thoughts. These were her father's men. Despite her anger at him, she knew she needed to choose her words carefully. Besides, she doubted these men would care much about Alice, anyway.

"My father, um, Captain Hook, and I traveled to get my friend Alice," said Rommy.

"What's that? I can't hears ya! Speak up, gal," said Stubbs, thumping his peg leg on the deck for emphasis.

Rommy started again, louder this time. "Papa and I meant to collect Alice from Chief Hawk Eye. She came with me to Neverland, and," Rommy looked over at Tommy, "no, she isn't my sister. How we met isn't really important. What is important is that when we were close to the encampment, we saw Tiger Lily sneaking away with Alice. Papa, um, the Captain, decided to follow Tiger Lily rather than stop her because he believed she would lead him to Pan." Rommy paused and breathed deeply as the crew muttered to each other. She could feel her anger stirring again, but it wouldn't do to show it before the crew.

"We followed her to the big willow, and Papa was right. Tiger Lily was taking Alice to Pan. Papa tried to ambush Pan, but, unfortunately, the crocodile chose that moment to attack. It was quite close, but Papa leapt onto the tree before the crocodile could hurt him. Pan took that opportunity to take Alice away with him."

"What're ya doin' back here iffen the Cap'n is stuck up a tree?" asked a gruff voice. It was the bald man she remembered from her first day aboard the ship. He hadn't looked very friendly before, and that hadn't changed. "Seems ta me, you shoulda been helpin', not flittin' back here caterwaulin' like a babe in arms." The man stepped closer to Rommy, a glower on his face.

"Now then, Corelli," said Gentleman Jack, slapping the man on his bare shoulder. "Let's give the young lady some slack, shall we? She's just lost her little friend, and I'm sure she's upset.

I don't think her experiences with Pan, or Neverland, for that matter, have been very pleasant up until now."

The man named Corelli snorted. "Pleasant ain't really the point, now is it? This ain't some school girl outing," he said. "I'd like to know what the Cap'n is thinkin', bringing a girlie onto the ship anyways. Iffen she twas my girl, I'da thrashed her but good and shipped 'er back where she come from. Seems he's gettin' a mite soft, is the Cap'n."

Murmuring swept through the men, and the air suddenly felt charged.

Gentleman Jack let out a bark of laughter. "Well, we can all be glad you've got such an ugly mug, and there's no danger of you having a daughter, Corelli," he said and flashed a grin.

Laughter rippled through the group of men, and the dark mood broke.

Gentleman Jack put his hand on her shoulder again. "Now, she's answered all your questions, men. Smee, why don't you take her to the Captain's quarters for a rest. I'll take a few of the men and head down to drive off that beast. It does have an unseemly interest in the Captain ever since it took off his hand."

Smee bustled up to her, taking her elbow. "Gentleman Jack's right, he is. Let's get you tucked up into the Captain's quarters, my dear. You've had a hard time of it, from all appearances. Poor lamb." Smee patted her hand as he led her from the deck back toward her father's cabin. Rommy followed him without protest. The men were still looking at her, and Corelli's calculated stare made a shiver run up her back.

Once inside the cabin, Smee gently pushed her into a chair before the small, pot-bellied stove. He knelt and stoked the embers of the fire so they came back to life. Then he put on the teakettle.

He smiled at her. "A spot of tea is what you need to put color back into those cheeks," he said.

Rommy let him fuss over her. It didn't take long before she had a blanket tucked around her legs and she held a steaming cup of tea in her hands.

"There, now," Smee said. He looked around with an air of satisfaction. "You just rest yerself. You're plumb wore out. I don't know why you and the Captain had to leave so early after all the fuss last night." He tsked disapprovingly as he walked toward the door, shaking his head. "I don't know what either of you were thinking," he said as he sailed out the door.

Rommy stared at the tea in her hand. She was still furious with her father and worried about Alice. But beneath all that was a heavy sadness. She had come so far, but had anything really changed?

She had screwed up her courage to sneak out of her boarding school after her father failed to show up for her birthday. Her mind retraced her steps from Chattingham's to getting lost in the London slums and meeting Alice. Then there was Finn. He had told her about Neverland and that her father was a pirate. She hadn't wanted to believe him, not her Papa! But Finn was right—about all of it. Even her father.

Pan's words came back to haunt her. Papa had lied to her about who he was. He had hidden his life in Neverland, and he had been so caught up in trying to use the Lost Boys to smoke out Pan, he had forgotten all about her.

Rommy shook her head. Once again, her father's need for revenge had been more important than she was. To be fair, when Pan had tied her up on the rock in Mermaid Lagoon, her father had let the Lost Boys go. He had been ready to come find her, not knowing she had escaped with a little help from a mermaid. She knew he loved her, but his desire for revenge was always there, and even after losing Alice, he wouldn't tell her why.

It was true. She had found her papa, but she still had no real answers. Why had Papa come to this island? Why was revenge so important that he had spent years chasing after Pan? Rommy set her teacup down and crossed her arms, resting her chin on them. When her father came back, she hoped he would answer her questions. He had to. Because if he didn't, Rommy wasn't sure she wanted to stay.

Chapter 6:
Papa's Confession

"**A**ndromeda!"

Rommy jerked her head off the table and blinked at her father, who stood in the doorway, scowling. Her head felt stuffed with cotton, and her eyes were gritty from crying.

Hook took one glance at her red, swollen eyes, and the stern expression on his face softened. He strode across the room. Pulling a chair around, he straddled it so his arms were resting on the back. He gave her a long look.

"What were you thinking, just flying off like that?" he said. "This is not some dreamland. There are dangerous things here. I know you were upset about Alice, but you really can't just take off whenever you get angry with me."

Rommy pushed herself up and straightened her shoulders. "I'm perfectly aware of the dangers of this island, Papa. I'm not a little girl."

"Well, you are *my* little girl, and I don't want anything to happen to you."

"What about other little girls? Like Alice." Rommy's chin jutted out. Her anger sparked to life again.

Hook sat back and raked his hook through his hair. "You don't understand, Andromeda... Rommy. Do you know how

24

many times I've almost had him? I've been so close, but he always manages to slither away. If there was any chance I could get Pan, I had to take it."

"Oh, I know how much you want to get Pan, but what I don't understand is why, Papa?" said Rommy leaning forward. "Why are you even here? You said Pan took something from you. What was it? Why is getting revenge more important than Alice?" She looked down at her hands. "More important than me?"

Hook jerked his head back, shock on his face. "Is that what you assume? That you aren't important to me?" He reached over and covered one of her hands with his. "Look at me, Rommy." Reluctantly, Rommy lifted her head and met his eyes. He squeezed her hand. "You are the most important person in the world to me, Rommy. You must trust me when I say that."

"It's hard to accept that, Papa, when I've spent most of my life only seeing you twice a year." Rommy looked away from her father and down at his hand gripping hers. "I wish...I wish you would come back to London and that we could be a regular family. I don't want you to stay here anymore. Let's rescue Alice and go home." As she said the word home, Rommy realized she didn't really have one, not with her father at any rate. She felt the prickle of tears and blinked rapidly, but one tear escaped and splashed onto her father's hand.

Hook blew out a breath. "I can't. We'll rescue your Alice, but...I can't leave here, not until Pan is gone."

"Then at least tell me why. I think I deserve to know what's so important that it's taken you away most of my life, and why you risked Alice today." Rommy pressed her lips together to

stop their trembling and looked back up. "If something happens to her, Papa, I...I...I don't know if I can forgive you."

Hook let go of her hand and rubbed his face. "It's a long
story and difficult to tell."

Rommy crossed her arms. "I'm not going anywhere."

Hook frowned, and after a long moment, nodded once.
"Maybe it's time then."

He rose from his chair and moved toward the back of the
cabin behind the screen where his bed was. She could hear him
rummaging around in the small chest of drawers with the cub-
bies on top.

"Blast, where is it?" she heard him say and then the sounds
of furniture scraping. A few moments later, he reemerged, a
photograph in his hand.

"I don't know how this got underneath the bed," he said
and placed the picture on the table. Rommy pulled the photograph toward her, already knowing what she would see. It was
the photo she had found just before Pan had attacked the ship
last night. In it, her father stood behind a woman who looked
like an older version of Rommy herself. On her lap sat a chubby
infant with a head of dark curls.

Rommy raised her eyes from the photo and met her father's
gaze. The anguish twisting his features shocked her. For a moment, guilt washed over Rommy for pushing him into talking
about this. Whatever had happened, it was still painful for her
father, that was plain to see.

"You've always told me Mama died when I was born," she
said slowly.

Hook nodded his head. "She did."

"Then, who is this?" Rommy asked, pointing to the baby.

"That was your brother, Sebastian."

"My brother? I have a brother? Where is he? Why have I never met him? Is he a Lost Boy?" Rommy's questions tumbled over each other in her excitement. She'd always been envious of all Francie's siblings.

"You did have a brother, Rommy, but he died." Hook turned the chair around and sat down heavily. "Right here on this island."

"What happened, Papa?" Rommy leaned toward him.

Hook's eyes were haunted as he stared into the past, and his voice was expressionless as he began his story. "Your mother and I were picnicking in Covington Gardens. Camilla loved the flowers there. Sebastian was about five, and we were expecting you. Your brother was playing, and then he was just gone. We searched and searched, but he had disappeared."

Hook paused and swallowed. "The only thing we found was his slingshot. He carried it with him everywhere. Next to it was a pile of sparkling dust." Hook shook his head, his face gray and drawn. "We called a constable, and there was a great search. The authorities helped us comb the gardens from one end to the other, but Sebastian was just gone. The only clue we had was another child, who claimed a boy dressed in a brown tunic and green leggings flew up to Sebastian and pulled him into the bushes."

"It was Pan, wasn't it?" breathed Rommy, her eyes wide.

"At the time, nobody took this child seriously, including me. A flying boy? It seemed impossible. We finally went back home, not knowing what else to do."

Hook's voice caught, and he cleared it before continuing. "I had to almost carry your mother away. She didn't want to leave in case our boy turned up or someone came forward. When she did finally consent to go home, she kept pacing to the window, looking out to see if anyone was coming with news. I eventually convinced her to lie down, but it was too late. The upset brought on her labor pains too early. You were born five weeks before the doctor had predicted. It didn't matter. You shouted your arrival to the world for everyone to hear." A slight smile curved Hook's mouth, and he gently touched Rommy's cheek. "Your mother got to see you, but she died soon afterwards. The doctor said it was her weak heart, but I will always believe that losing Sebastian was too much for her fragile health, and it killed her."

"But how did you find out about Neverland? How did you even get here?" Rommy asked, leaning toward her father.

Hook straightened and dashed a hand across his eyes. "It wasn't easy, but I had to know what happened. It felt like a clock was ticking inside of me, and Sebastian's time was running out. The only clues I had were the child's story about the flying boy and the pile of sparkling dust. It took a lot of searching, and keep in mind I had you at home. You had a nanny, but I didn't want to let you too far out of my sight. You were the only thing I had left in this world." Hook's voice became rough, but he continued. "I hunted down any rumor or story about a flying boy or the sparkling dust. The answers finally led me to an old man who owned a bookshop just off Piccadilly Square. It's a small place, and I'm not sure if it still exists. The man was quite elderly when I first talked to him, and that was at least 10 years ago. He told me about Neverland and a lad named Peter Pan. I didn't believe him at first, but I was out of options."

"However did you get to Neverland, though? I thought grown-ups couldn't fly."

"You have to understand, Rommy, I was desperate," said Hook. "I trapped several of the fairies that inhabit a few of the gardens around London. I took their pixie dust and forced them to show me how to get here."

From her father's expression, Rommy realized she didn't want to know how he had done that. "Did you see Sebastian? Did you find him?" Rommy was perched on the edge of her seat now, intent on her father's answers.

Hook deflated into his chair as if someone had leaked the life out of him. "No, no, I didn't. I was too late. He was already dead. There was another pirate captain before I came here. Sebastian died in a battle Pan had with that man and his crew."

"No," Rommy cried. Even though she knew her brother was dead, part of her had been expecting a different ending.

"Unfortunately, he had died only a short time before I found Neverland." Hook's good hand curled into a fist, and his voice was rough. "I'll never forgive myself for not getting here more quickly, for not believing that child's story sooner. As it was, it took over a year before I discovered this place existed or how to get here."

Rommy jumped from her chair and threw her arms around her father. "Oh Papa, it wasn't your fault! How could you have guessed all this even existed?"

Her father's arms squeezed her back. "He was my son. I should have found a way, but I didn't. Now, do you understand why I can't rest until Pan pays for his deeds?"

Rommy squeezed her father tighter and nodded. Silently, she promised herself that somehow, someway, she would help Papa make this right.

Chapter 7:
Musings in the Riggings

Rommy sat among the rigging, staring at the photograph of her father, mother, and the brother she hadn't known existed until just a few hours ago.

Far below her on the deck, she could see her father's men moving around the deck like so many mice. Snatches of songs and voices filtered up to her perch, but the whistling wind muffled the sounds.

Her father had made it clear he didn't want her around the crew, and after her run-in with Corelli, she almost saw his point. Besides, after his revelations, Rommy didn't feel much like talking to anyone.

With a finger, she traced the face of the chubby infant in the picture. While her father and mother looked serious in the picture, the baby's face was wreathed in smiles. It was no wonder her father was so bent on revenge. Rommy understood now why her father was so driven to get rid of Pan.

She sighed. Once they had retrieved Alice, the chances of talking her father into returning to London and of giving up this quest seemed remote now. A thought had wormed its way to the front of her mind and wouldn't leave her alone. Why was his revenge for her brother's death more important than she was? He had said she was the most important person in the world to him, but it didn't feel that way.

Rommy immediately felt guilty. She remembered the anguish on Papa's face when he spoke of his son and wife. Until a short while ago, she didn't even know Sebastian had existed, so in all honesty, it was difficult to mourn him. She had always wanted a sibling, but she couldn't pretend sorrow for someone she had never met. And even with Mama, it was more the idea of having a mother she missed. After all, Camilla Cavendish had died only hours after Rommy's birth. It was hard to miss someone you didn't know.

Rommy stood up on the wooden beam, put the picture into her trouser pocket, and looked toward the bow of the boat. Her father was talking to Smee, his hook flashing as he gestured.

A sadness weighed her down, and she realized the person she missed the most, the one she mourned for, was the one still alive—her father. The sadness pressed down on her harder. Rommy, after years of relying on herself, had a practical streak. She realized with a certainty she couldn't shake that her father would never really be a true part of her life until Papa defeated Pan or let the idea of revenge go. She doubted that would ever happen. She blinked back tears as the hopelessness of it all washed over her.

She reached up a hand to wipe the tears away when suddenly a glowing ball of light appeared in front of her face. Rommy recognized the creature as a fairy, but it wasn't Nissa, the fairy that always seemed to be flittering around Finn. This one wore a tiny iridescent dress that shimmered between green and blue. Her black hair floated around her small pointed face, and big green eyes blinked at Rommy. The tiny creature hovered in front of her face and pulled something dark out of a minuscule bag it carried. She thrust it into Rommy's face, and when Rommy closed her hand around the object, she felt something crackle. When she opened her hand, a single dark curl lay in her hand along with a small piece of parchment. Cold dread bloomed in her stomach, and her hands trembled as she smoothed out the paper.

Come to the caves alone, and Alice can go free. If you don't come, the next thing I send won't be a curl. You have until sunrise. Peter

"What caves?" Rommy asked, but the fairy had disappeared while she was reading. Her knees turned wobbly, and she sank back down on the wooden beam. What was she going to do? What would she tell Papa? He'd never let her go alone, but if he didn't...

Suddenly a face appeared in front of her. The face was upside down. Rommy blinked at it in confusion and quickly closed her hand to hide the curl and paper.

"Hi!" The face disappeared and then Max was standing next to her, grinning. He balanced on the end of the beam with only blue sky around him, but he looked relaxed.

His smile slid away when he saw her reddened eyes. "Hey, what's wrong?" he asked.

Rommy felt her cheeks burn. She hated crying, and it was so embarrassing that this young man would catch her at it. After her breakdown on the deck earlier, he must think her some kind of watering pot.

She forced a smile. "Nothing at all. The wind is just making my eyes water is all. It's Max, right?"

"That's my name, alright," he said cheerfully. "I was to let you know the Cap'n, he's wanting you in his cabin for dinner soon. Nobody saw where'd ya gone, but I thought to myself, if I wanted to have spell to myself, I'd come on up here."

Max took a deep breath and looked out at the Cove's blue waters. "Something about being up here, it clears the head, it does." He smiled down at her and then clapped her on the shoulder, almost sending her spinning off her perch. "Best get moving, though. The Cap'n, he ain't much fer waiting." He paused and gazed into her face. "Are you sure you're all right?"

Rommy forced a smile. "Yes, I'm good. Thank you. I'll be down soon, I promise."

Max smiled and with a wink, he dropped off the beam and out of sight. Rommy stared at the space where he had been and peered down. He had already scrambled halfway down the mast.

Despite his words, Rommy didn't leave just yet. She looked out across the Cove. The sun was getting low in the sky, and a glow was spreading over the waters. It was beautiful, but beneath all that beauty, there lurked something deadly on this island, magic or not. And now she needed to walk into that danger with or without her father's permission.

Chapter 8:
Dinner with Papa

Rommy sat across from her father. He had taken off his coat, and the lace cuffs of his shirt threatened to drag in his plate. As she watched Papa wincing as he lifted his fork to his mouth, she realized that his missing hand was a bigger issue than she had thought. When he showed up at school that first time sporting a silver hook instead of a hand, she had been horrified. Hook had been quick to assure her he was just fine, and she had accepted it. Now she understood that wasn't the only struggle he had hidden from her. She shifted in her chair and the paper in her pocket crinkled. Papa wasn't the only one hiding things anymore.

Her father looked up from his food and smiled. "What is it, my dear?" he asked.

She shrugged and forced a smile onto her face. "I was just remembering yesterday at this time there was a mad battle going on." She gestured at her plate with sliced beef, fried potatoes and creamed peas. "I think I prefer this."

Hook chuckled. "It's much better than battling Pan and those Lost Boys of his." A look of distaste crossed his face, but he smoothed it away. He lifted another forkful of beef to his mouth.

Rommy looked around the cabin. Smee had put a cloth over the worn table and a merry fire crackled in the potbelly stove. The lanterns had been lit, so a warm glow fell over the space.

Hook had cleared most of his plate, but Rommy had only taken a few bites. "Is the food not to your liking, my dear?" he asked.

"Oh no, Papa," said Rommy, focusing back on her plate with a guilty flush, very aware of the note and the lock of hair in her pocket. "I was just thinking, so much has happened. It's hard to take it all in now that things are quiet."

Hook put down his fork and patted his mouth with a napkin. "You have had quite a few shocks over the past few days, haven't you? How are you...that is to say...I'm sure Alice must be on your mind and...and all the other things we talked about." Hook cleared his throat and rolled his big shoulders.

Rommy hesitated and looked down at her plate, away from her father's piercing gaze. Now would be the time to tell him about Pan's note, to ask for his help. How could she possibly outsmart Pan when he was expecting her and she was walking onto his territory? It seemed impossible all by herself, but Papa had the whole crew at his disposal. She looked up at her father's expectant face, and the failed rescue attempt that morning flashed through her mind. Could she trust him? Would he even let her go this time?

She put down the fork she had been using to push her food back and forth. "I'm glad your real life isn't a secret anymore, and that you told me about my brother and what really happened to Mama," she said. She shrugged. "But it's just...I guess

I need to get used to it, is all." She paused. "And I'm worried about Alice."

Her father cleared his throat again and rearranged his fork on his plate. "Yes, well, I was talking about that to Smee earlier." He leaned forward. "We need to find where Pan is holed up before we can come up with any kind of plan."

"When he had Alice and me, he was in those caves, the ones at the base of the cliff on the far side of the island." Rommy gestured with her hands. "The one where the waterfall is."

Hook steepled his hand over his hook. "Hmm, maybe I should send one of my men to scout it out, to see if he's still there. Once we learn where he has Alice, we can mount a surprise attack." A smile spread across Hook's face. "And who knows? Perhaps we can catch more than one fish in our net."

Rommy's hopes popped like a soap bubble at his words, and she shook her head. "No, Papa! We already lost Alice once." She leaned forward and grabbed his arm. "Promise me that when we go after her you won't be just using it as a way to get Pan, not this time."

Hook patted her hand but his eyes slid away from hers. "Of course, my dear. Little Alice will be our top priority. Don't you worry. I'll bring my best men, and we'll have her back before you know it." He straightened his cuffs. "If we happen to catch Pan, too, well, that will just be a happy bonus."

Rommy's stomach sank at his words. She was on her own tonight.

"Now," said Hook, in a determinedly jovial tone, "eat your dinner because I have a surprise for you."

"A surprise? I'm not sure if I want anymore of those," Rommy said, meaning every word.

Hook gave a bark of laughter. "I can promise you, this is one you'll like, my dear. So, hurry and eat up."

It didn't take long for Rommy to clean most of her plate. When she set down her fork, her father jumped up and held out his good hand to her.

"Now then," he said, "you are a young lady, and you'll soon have Alice with you. I talked with Smee, and we both agreed that it would be best for you to have your own cabin during your time on the ship."

"But, I thought you had the only cabin, Papa," said Rommy. "Don't your men all sleep down below decks?"

Clasping her hand and pulling her toward the door, Hook said, "Yes, most of the men do sleep in the hold below decks, but Smee has his own cabin. It's much smaller than mine, but he's agreed to give it up for the duration of your visit." Her father beamed at her. "I think you'll find it comfortable."

"But Papa, I can't take Mr. Smee's bed all summer. Wherever will he sleep?"

"Why, down in the hold with the other men," said her father.

"But..."

Hook waved her objections away and said, "He's glad to do it. I've never seen a man so besotted. He would probably try to hang the moon if you asked him, my dear." Her father leaned down. "If I didn't know better, I might doubt his loyalty if it came down to you or me." Her father winked at her.

Rommy forced a smile and let her father lead her out of his cabin and around the corner. What she had assumed was entirely her father's quarters, was really two cabins. Smee's small cabin hugged the side of the Captain's. Hook opened a small, hidden door and gestured inside. Although a fifth the size of her father's cabin, it was still clean and cozy. An old, worn quilt covered the bed in the corner, a trunk at its foot. A tiny potbellied stove was near the wall the two cabins shared. Rommy realized its twin was just on the other side of the paneled wall. A small, squat chair crouched in front of the miniature stove. In the opposite corner stood a small washbasin.

She turned to her father. "It's perfect, Papa. I'll be quite comfortable here. I must thank Mr. Smee," she said. In truth, Rommy couldn't help thinking that for once, her father's timing was perfect.

"He's occupied at the moment, but I'll pass your thanks along," said Hook. "He was tickled to do it for you. Why don't you make yourself comfortable? Smee's washed some of your clothes and put them in that trunk, along with a few of my shirts you can use as nightclothes. Would you like me to have Stubbs bring you the bathing tub?"

Rommy glanced down at her clothes. They were the ones Smee had commandeered from someone this morning, she wasn't sure who. The earlier clash with Pan had left them creased and grimy. A bath would give her time to think of a plan without being under her father's watchful gaze.

"That sounds wonderful," she said. She didn't have to force her smile. A bath really did sound wonderful.

Her father took a step toward the door, and then he turned and swept her into a tight hug. "You know how important you are to me, don't you?" he said into her hair.

Rommy felt tears well up in her eyes as she hugged him back. She nodded her head. "Yes, Papa," she said. "I know."

Chapter 9:
Rommy's Decision

Rommy lay in the little bed listening to the creak of the ship and the sounds of the crew as things wound down for the night. She was still wearing her father's shirt, which enveloped her in billows of fabric down to her shins. She absently played with the damp braid lying over her shoulder. Waiting was difficult, especially since all she could think of were the many ways this rescue attempt could go wrong.

Papa had already tucked her in quite a while ago, but Rommy knew it was entirely possible he might check on her before going to bed himself. If she got dressed too soon, the jig was up.

The coming confrontation with Pan turned over and over in her mind. There had to be a way for her to rescue Alice, but still not end up Pan's hostage. While his note had said he'd let Alice go if she came, Rommy was under no delusions of how trustworthy Pan was.

Finally, she couldn't stand it any longer and sat up, swinging her legs off the bed. Tiptoeing to the door, she opened it and peeked her head out. Since the cabin door faced the side of the ship, she didn't have a good view of the main deck. From here, it appeared quiet, but she'd have to get a closer look to be sure. If anyone asked what she was doing, she could claim she was looking for a chamber pot or something.

Hugging the cabin wall, she padded forward until she had reached the front corner. The deck was mostly empty. Lanterns hung from various places, their wicks trimmed for the night. She knew there was probably at least one man up in the crow's nest, but he wasn't likely to be looking down. Rommy stared toward the bow of the boat. She could see no movement from here. She let out a breath of relief. It looked like her father had turned in for the night.

Just as this thought crossed her mind, the door to her father's cabin opened, spilling a square of light onto the shadowy deck. She jerked back, pressing herself against the cabin wall.

Smee backed out. "Yes, Captain," he said. "I'll just look in on her on my way below decks. The darling girl must be plumb tuckered out." He chuckled. "She's certainly had a busy few days."

Rommy heard the growl of her father's voice, and Smee bobbed his head up and down. "Yes, sir, of course, sir. You are exactly right; it isn't anything to laugh about."

Rommy didn't wait but ran back to her own cabin. She rushed through the door on bare feet and forced herself to pull the door shut softly, even though everything in her was screaming at her to hurry.

She slipped into the bed and pulled the covers to her chin, shutting her eyes just as the door cracked back open. She didn't dare move or even breathe. There was a pause, and then Smee sighed. The door clicked shut a moment later.

Rommy let out the breath she was holding and lay there for a long moment before sitting up and swinging her legs over the side of the bed. The room was dark, the only lantern turned down to a mere flicker. Moving silently through the shadowy darkness, Rommy pulled her nightgown over her head and slipped into the shirt and breeches Smee had found for her. She thought they were Tommy's, since he was the only person on this boat remotely near to her own size, but the clothes were still too big. She was just thankful that she could wear breeches instead of being forced to mount a rescue expedition in a dress and petticoats.

Rommy wanted nothing more than to dash out the door, but caution made her pause. Just because Smee had checked on her didn't mean he had gone below decks just yet. She sat on the edge of her bed, beating out a rhythm with her feet. Slowly she counted to 500 before walking over to the door and cracking it open.

The space outside her door was empty. She stuck her head out, and a thought hit her. What if her father, or even Smee, checked on her again during the night? Her father didn't seem to sleep all that much. It wouldn't do to raise the alarm too early. Hurriedly, she knelt by the trunk and pulled out her other shirt and breeches. Rolling them into a bundle, she stuffed them under the quilt. She arranged the pillow to look like someone was lying on it.

She looked at the bed critically. If anyone just peeked in, it would appear like someone were sleeping in the bed. With any luck, her father or Smee wouldn't look any closer.

With quiet steps, Rommy slipped out of her cabin again and sneaked toward the back of the boat. Once again, she realized how much flying came in handy when trying to sneak off somewhere. It certainly would have made leaving Chattingham's loads easier. She stifled a giggle, imagining her and Francie flying out their bedroom window.

She glanced around one more time before she slid over the railing and floated down the side of the boat. She would have to stay close to the water and maybe go around the long way so nobody in the crow's nest would see her.

Rommy sunk toward the small waves that were lapping at the hull of the boat. She remembered the long, difficult path she had walked when she had first found her father's ship. The entire route would take twice as long, but she knew she'd be visible to anyone on deck if she went the shorter way. Edging out past the side of the boat, she focused on a rocky section that wouldn't be too far from the more open riverbank. Suddenly, she was yanked backward. She opened her mouth to scream, but a hand clamped over it.

Chapter 10:
Finn Has a Plan

Bucking and twisting, Rommy kicked at her captor, trying to get her teeth into the hand over her mouth.

"Knock it off! It's me, Finn," said a voice close to her ear. She stopped thrashing and felt his arm loosen, and the hand disappeared from her mouth. She whirled to face him, shocked at how easily he had snuck up on her.

"What are you doing here?" she whispered. "If my father or his men see you, we'll both be in a trouble."

He smirked. "Don't worry about me," he said. "I've had lots of practice not being seen. After all, I followed you for over a year and you never saw me, not once!"

Rommy felt her cheeks redden, reminded that despite his help on several occasions, Finn had been spying on her. She'd do well to remember the original reason he brought her to Neverland was as bait to get her father to let the Lost Boys go.

"You still didn't answer my question—what are you doing here?" Getting Finn to answer questions was like trying to nail down a moonbeam.

He flashed a grin. "Just think of me as your escort," he said.

"Escort? What are you talking about?"

"He sent me to make sure you didn't sneak up on him or bring anyone with you."

"How'd he even know I'd come?" Rommy asked.

"Pan knew you'd come for Alice," said Finn. He grimaced. "He said you had to be the hero; you couldn't help it."

"If by that he means I can't let someone I care about come to harm, well, I guess he's right," said Rommy, lifting her chin.

Finn held out his hands. "Look, don't get mad at me. I'm just telling you what he said."

Rommy rolled her eyes. "Maybe you should consider being more than Pan's mouthpiece," she said.

"Hey, there's no need to get nasty," said Finn, crossing his arms. "And for your information, Miss Know-It-All, I have a plan to help you and Alice get away. I don't want to see you or Alice get hurt, either." Finn looked up toward the deck of the boat and tipped his head toward the shoreline. "We need to get away from this boat, and then I can tell you what I'm thinking."

Rommy hated to agree with him, but he was right. The longer she was gone, the more chance there was that someone would notice. It was one thing if her father caught her, but it would be entirely different if he found her with Finn. As annoying as he could be, she'd rather not see Papa impale Finn with his hook or something.

"Follow me," Finn said and flitted across the water toward the far shore. Rommy followed at his heels, expecting at any moment for a shout to come from her father's ship, but nobody noticed them zipping over the waves.

The two landed behind an outcropping of rocks. Rommy turned to face Finn. "Do you truly expect Alice and I can both get away?" she asked. "I've been thinking and thinking, and I haven't come up with a way to get the better of Pan if he knows I'm coming."

"Of course you can't," Finn said, smirking again. Rommy felt an itch to slap it off of his face but controlled the impulse. "You just need a little help from your friends, or rather my friends."

Before Rommy could ask any more questions, Finn motioned to her and they picked their way along the rocky shoreline. Once they were in the sky again, Finn told her the rest of his plan.

"Look, you're not the only one who thinks Pan is kinda off his feed around here," he said. "Most of the people and creatures on the island want to stay on Pan's good side, but that doesn't mean they like him."

"If they don't like him, why would they help you?" asked Rommy.

Finn spun to face her, flying backwards. "Because, as Pan's, what did you call me—mouthpiece—he sends me to smooth things over all the time, and I've made friends with everyone."

He tapped his upper lip and added, "Sometimes, I figure that's one of the only reasons Pan doesn't get rid of me. He knows I keep the balance on this island from tipping against him."

Finn returned to his spot next to her, and the two flew onward. "That might be, but how will your friends help us exactly?" Rommy asked.

Finn grinned again. "The big question is, are you a good swimmer?"

The question so surprised Rommy that she stopped mid-air. "What has that got to do with anything?"

Finn came back to hover beside her. "Just answer the question," he said.

Rommy huffed out a breath. "Yes, we had swimming at Chattingham's. Why is that so important?"

Finn nodded. "Good. When my friends provide the distraction, you and Alice have swim underneath the waterfall. There's a tunnel that will take you out to the far side of the cliffs. You can circle around and get back to the boat that way."

"Won't Pan know about that tunnel and be suspicious? Won't he be watching for us to come back?"

Finn grinned, his gray eyes sparkling. "Not if I point him in the wrong direction, he won't. Besides, he doesn't know about that tunnel. Nissa showed it to me. Like I said, a lot of the fairies aren't too fond of Pan."

Rommy grabbed Finn's arm. "But what if he finds out you tricked him? Pan seems like the type to hold a grudge. Won't that put you in danger?"

"Don't worry, it'll be okay," said Finn. He put his hand on top of hers.

Rommy's eyes flew up to his, and for a moment Finn looked like he had swallowed something the wrong way. Then his cocky grin returned.

"Awww, don't tell me you're worried about me," he said, pulling his hand away and giving her a playful shove. "I know how to get around old Pan."

The tension in her shoulders eased, and relief spread through Rommy. She had been willing to sacrifice herself for Alice. But knowing that she had Finn on her side—and apparently his friends, too—gave her hope that this wouldn't be a huge disaster.

As the two continued flying, a thought hit Rommy. "What is Pan planning on doing with me, anyway? I assume this has to do with getting to my father and perhaps revenge because I beat him in our fight." She paused and swallowed. "Is he going to try to...kill me?"

Finn's face darkened and a frown replaced his grin. He seemed to pick his words carefully. "Pan gets, I don't know, fixed on things and people sometimes, and he's fixed on you. Oh sure, he wants to use you to get to your father, but it's more than that." Finn glanced at her. "He's convinced he can get you to join him."

"Join him? Is he crazy? No, don't answer that," Rommy said and shook her head. "I would think it would be clear by now there's no chance of that happening."

"Yeah, well, Pan gets crazier every day, and there's no talking him out of something once he's decided it's what he wants. Just be careful. He gets vicious if he doesn't get what he wants."

Rommy rolled her eyes. "Yeah, I kind of realized that."

Finn chuckled. "I guess you would, wouldn't you?"

As the two flew onward to the meeting with Pan, Rommy turned this new information over her mind. On the one hand, it was rather nerve-racking to realize she was Pan's new focus, but maybe—just maybe—she could use that to her advantage.

Chapter 11:

So, We Meet Again

Rommy and Finn landed on the riverbank and hunkered down in the tall grass. Up ahead, the cliffs loomed. She could see where the water tumbled over the cliff face and splashed down into a deep pool before taking off again in the river.

To one side of the churning pool and in front of the cliff face, a fire crackled merrily. Various rocks and branches circled around it like so many chairs. Boys of various sizes slouched on or tumbled around them, laughing and shouting. Flute music floated on the breeze.

This was it. A weight settled in Rommy's stomach. Finn looked at her. "Remember, follow my lead, and look for that distraction," he said.

"How will I know?" Rommy asked.

Finn grinned. "Oh, you'll know," he said.

Rommy felt an answering grin spread across her face. The two lifted off the ground, and Finn clamped a hand on her arm. She looked at him in surprise.

"Escort, remember?"

She nodded and let him pull her forward. As they drew near the group, her stomach clenched. She just hoped this went the way they had planned.

Pan heard them before anyone else, and a smile spread across his face and he lowered the instrument he was playing. Rommy shivered as she and Finn landed at the edge of the circle of light thrown from the fire.

Squaring her shoulders and taking a deep breath, Rommy stepped into the firelight, Finn still hanging onto her arm. "I'm here," she said. "Now where's Alice?"

The laughter and voices immediately fell silent as a dozen pair of eyes all swiveled in her direction.

Pan crowed in delight and pushed up from the rock that he was lounging against. "I knew you'd come," he said. He looked around at the circle of boys. "Didn't I say she'd come? And I was right!"

A small, dirty boy with dark hair and golden eyes piped up. "You're always right, Peter. It's why you're the leader."

"He ain't always right," said a boy with light brown hair. He was built square and thick. "He said we would beat ole Captain Hook, but then a girl..." The boy next to him, who looked like his mirror image, hit him and shook his head, but it was too late.

Pan was already hovering in front the speaker; a small, lethal-looking dagger was in his hand. "What's that you said, Charlie?" He leaned close to the boy and flicked at the button on the boy's tunic with the knife. The boy swallowed hard and mumbled, "Nothin'."

Pan cocked his head. "No, Charlie, speak up, since you're so smart." The boy remained mute, staring at his bare feet.

Pan smirked and pointed at the smaller boy who had spoken. "I always knew you were a smart one, Willie. Not like old Charlie over here. He's full of beans." Still looking at Willie, Pan's hand snaked out and drove the dagger into the tree immediately behind Charlie's head. A thin trickle of blood appeared on the boy's cheek. He didn't move to wipe it away.

All the boys laughed, but the sound was uneasy.

Rommy's eyes roamed around the circle of faces. She recognized the white-blond hair that belonged to Walter. A boy perched on one of the larger rocks had a small creature curled up on his shoulder. His guarded dark eyes watched her from under a fringe of black hair.

Another boy, his hair a dirty blond, hung back, shifting from foot to foot. He chewed on his thumbnail. His hazel eyes looked worried rather than watchful.

"Are you Hook's daughter?" The small boy who asked had brilliant red hair and freckles covered his face. He bobbed up and down, unable to stand still. His bright green eyes were alive with curiosity.

She looked at the boy and nodded.

He hopped up and down and jerked on the arm of the boy standing next to him. This one seemed a bit older, and he was tall, his hair a sandy color. "Did you hear that, Oscar? She's Hook's daughter, the one that can fight like a boy. And she's going to be one us—a Lost Boy." The taller boy patted the redhead absently.

Rommy turned her eyes back to Pan who was watching her with a sly smile. "You said that if I came, you'd let Alice go. Now, where is she?" she asked.

Pan shook his head. "Here I was trying to welcome you, but you are always in such a hurry." He flew over to her, landing too close. Rommy had to fight not to step back from him. Instead, she lifted her chin.

Pan stared at where Finn's hand still rested on her arm. He raised an eyebrow. "I don't think she's going anywhere," he said.

Finn dropped his hand and took a step away from Rommy. He gave a laugh. "You never know with this one."

Pan chuckled. "Yes, our little Rommy is full of surprises." He patted her cheek, and it was all she could do not to shudder.

Instead, she lifted her chin a notch higher. "This is all very nice, Pan, but where is Alice? She's why I came, after all."

Pan looked over at the boy still chewing his fingernail. "Jem, go get our newest recruit." The boy flinched and then scuttled toward one of the caves.

Pan shrugged. "For some reason, Alice didn't want to join us tonight. We did invite her."

"I don't want to come out there," a familiar voice said. "I told you I ain't wantin' to be around that fruit loop."

"P-P-Pan says you gotta come," Jem said.

There was a scuffling sound, and then Jem dragged Alice from the cave, her hands tied in front of her. Her hair was a tangled nest on top of her head, and her dress's sleeve hung from her shoulder. A purple bruise bloomed across her cheek. Noticing it, Rommy clenched her fists.

Across the space, Rommy met Alice's eyes. She saw the relief in the younger girl's eyes. Alice pulled her arm from the boy's grasp and made a beeline toward Rommy. Pan intercepted her, dragging the little girl up close against his side. She leaned away from him, but he didn't let go.

"I told you that you should've joined us," he said. He ran his finger along the bruise on her cheek and made a tsking noise. "So stubborn, and you almost missed our visitor."

"Alice, are you okay?" Rommy asked.

The little girl nodded her head, but her eyes cut to Pan. She raised her eyebrows at Rommy. Rommy gave a barely perceptible nod of her head. The side of Alice's mouth flicked upward for a moment, and then she screwed up her face.

"You shouldn't have come!" said Alice. To Rommy's surprise, the girl blinked her eyes until two tears appeared and rolled down her cheeks. She bit the inside of her cheek. She had no idea Alice was such a good actor.

Rommy looked at Pan and spread out her arms. "You said you'd let Alice go if I came. Well, I'm here."

Pan smiled, and, without warning, shoved Alice away from him. She stumbled and almost fell. "Go on then," he said. "Nobody's keeping you here."

Rommy gritted her teeth. "Untie her. You know you can't send her out all by herself with her hands tied up. She'll never survive. You need to let Finn or another Lost Boy take her back to my father's ship."

Pan was suddenly nose-to-nose with Rommy. He smiled showing all of his teeth. "I said she could go free. I said nothing about how I'd let her go." He paused, and his eyes slitted. "Of course, she can always stay here with us. I can't say that I mind having Lost Girls instead of Lost Boys. They don't eat nearly as much."

One of the boys, she thought it was the one Pan had called Willie, laughed, holding his belly. "Good one, Peter!" he said.

The others ignored him, focused on the exchange between her and Pan.

Pan flew up into the air and hovered cross-legged. His eyes focused on Rommy when he spoke. "Well, Alice, what do you think? Do you want to stay or leave? This is the only time I'll ask."

Alice scowled up at him. "You always was a complete git," she said.

Pan laughed. "So much spirit," he said. He looked around at the boys. "I told you she'd made a good Lost Boy. She just needs to be trained." Then he swiveled toward Rommy and pointed. "And *she* will, too." He flew up beside her, his face sliding next to hers. "Will you need training too, Rommy?"

"I wanna see her fight," the redheaded boy said. He was jumping up and down again. Rommy briefly wondered if he ever stood still.

A light appeared in Pan's eyes as he whirled toward the little boy. "What a brilliant idea, Henry," he said. "Every Lost Boy gets an initiation. This will be perfect for Hook's daughter." He winked at Rommy. "I don't suppose you brought your sword with you?"

Rommy just stared back at Pan and held both arms out at her sides as an answer. She wanted to throttle that little red-haired boy. Her eyes found Finn. She hoped that whatever he was planning would happen soon. The last thing she wanted to do was get into a duel with Pan.

With Pan's focus on her, Finn had edged toward the darkness beyond the fire's circle of light. Now, he froze, a look of panic on his face. He wiped away the expression when Pan whirled toward him.

"Get my extra dirk," Pan said. He looked back at Rommy and shrugged. "I know you prefer your sword, but we have to use what we have."

Chapter 12:
Midnight Rescue

Rommy crossed her arms, playing for time. "What if I refuse?"

Pan shook his finger at her playfully. "I'd say that would be a fatal mistake." He let out a peal of laughter and spun away. Finn came out of a cave, holding a weapon that looked old and beaten up.

"Ah, here it is," said Pan. He plucked the short sword from Finn's hand and flew toward Rommy. He presented it to her hilt first. "It was my old man's, but when I left, he didn't need it anymore." A spasm of rage flickered across Pan's face, and Rommy flinched away from him. Noticing her reaction, Pan's face smoothed back into a smile, but it had a sharp edge to it. She reluctantly took the dirk from him.

Rommy swallowed. Finn could start that distraction anytime now. She looked around for Alice. Catching her eye, Alice gave a small nod. The little girl was rubbing the bindings on her wrists against a rock. Alice would be ready.

The Lost Boys had formed a circle, and Rommy and Pan were at the center. She wasn't sure when Finn would act, but she wasn't about to let Pan get the jump on her. She raised the sword and balanced on her toes.

Pan let out a loud laugh. "Look at that, boys," he said. "I knew our Rommy would not disappoint."

Without warning, he whirled and brought his dirk down in a savage arc. Rommy thrust up her own dirk and blocked him. The force sent vibrations up her arm and into her shoulders. Her focus narrowed onto Pan. Dimly, she could hear the boys shouting, but she concentrated on blocking and striking. The two of them whirled up off the ground in a dance of clashing steel.

Pan flitted away from her, and his laugh was full of joy. "I knew it," he said. "I knew you'd be brilliant with us."

Rommy lunged at him, and he blocked her at the last moment. "I'm not with you," she said through gritted teeth.

"Admit it," said Pan as he drove her backward with a flurry of strikes. "You want this; you want to be a part of this. Your old man does nothing but disappoint you."

Rommy halted his onslaught and went on an attack of her own. "I'm. Not. Joining. You." She punctuated each word with a slashing strike. Pan blocked them. His next lock put them almost face-to-face behind their weapons. He stared into her eyes before he shoved hard. They separated, both panting.

"If you win," he said, "you and Alice can go." He whirled around, and hot pain slashed across her arm as the tip of his sword sliced through the fabric of her shirt. He backed away and smiled at her. "But if you lose, you're mine."

Rommy's grip on her sword tightened. She didn't want to enter any bargains with Pan, but Finn had yet to produce that distraction. She gave a small nod. Pan rushed at her, holding his sword like a club. She dodged to the side, and he blew past her.

Her dirk darted out, and Pan hissed as her weapon drew a line on his forearm.

Before Pan could strike back, the sky was suddenly full of birds. Bright feathers flashed in the twinkling light from the stars, and the air filled with a loud cacophony of squawks and screeches.

Startled, Pan clapped his hands over his ears. Rommy hesitated. Pan's focus was on the birds flapping around him. He was completely vulnerable. Rommy could end this once and for all. The dirk trembled in her hand. She looked at his scrunched-up face with his eyes squeezed shut. He looked very young in that moment.

She threw down the dirk and whirled away, rocketing toward Alice who had gotten her hands free at last.

"We need to hurry, Alice." She pulled the little girl toward the water that glistened in the moonlight.

Alice dug in her heels. "What're ya doing? Shouldn't we be bunking it?" She thrust a thumb in the opposite direction.

"That's the first place Pan will look," said Rommy, tugging at the girl to get her to move.

As they got closer to the waterfall and the frothing pool at its base, Alice balked again. "Come on," urged Rommy. "Finn said there's a cave behind the waterfall and a tunnel."

"But I can't swim," said Alice, her face white.

Rommy stared at her in dismay. She glanced around. Finn was waving his hand to go. The birds continued to dart and dive, but she could see the boys were reacting now. Several had picked up stones and were throwing them. A few hit their mark. High above them, Pan was no longer stationary. She saw him point at Finn. "You!" Pan yelled.

There was no time left and no other options. Grabbing Alice's arm, Rommy said, "Hang on and don't let go." And then she leaped into the water, pulling Alice with her.

Rommy and Alice both sunk below the churning water. The girls surfaced, Alice sputtering and clutching onto Rommy like a wet cat.

"Alice," she said. The girl's fear-glazed eyes didn't seem to see her, so Rommy lightly slapped Alice's cheek. "Alice, if you keep clutching at me like that, we're both going to drown."

Alice seemed to snap back, but she was trembling. "It's okay," said Rommy. "Now, I need you to come around me so that you can hang onto my shoulders from the back. You just keep a tight grip on me, and I'll swim under the waterfall. It'll be over before you know it."

"Under the waterfall? Did yer mother drop you on yer head? You can't swim under a waterfall. It'll smash us to bits, it will!"

"It won't, Alice," said Rommy. "You have to trust me, or Pan's going to find us."

Alice's violet eyes stared into Rommy's, and she pressed her quivering lips together. "Okay," she said finally. The little girl inched her way around to Rommy's back. It seemed to take forever until her small hands clutched Rommy's shoulders.

"Take a deep breath, Alice," said Rommy over the roar of the waterfall. Following her own advice, Rommy filled her lungs and dove.

Within seconds, Rommy was being pummeled by the waterfall, the pressure pushing her toward the bottom of the pool with inexorable force. Alice's fingers dug into her shoulders. It was impossible to see through the churning water, and the force shoved Rommy's body from the force. Desperately, she moved what she hoped was forward through the roar of the water.

Her foot brushed the rocky bottom of the pool, and then she felt a searing pain. Her left calf was on fire, but she kept swimming. And then they were through. She surfaced inside a cavern that lay in inky blackness. Moonlight filtered through the rushing water and barely illuminated the cave's interior. She paddled over to the edge of the pool. Alice peeled her hands off Rommy's shoulders and pulled herself up onto the bank. Rommy flopped next to her.

She twisted around and stared at her leg. It was difficult to see in the cave's darkness. She rolled up her pant leg, hissing in pain.

"What is it?" Alice asked, crawling closer.

"I think something bit me," said Rommy, peering at two puncture marks surrounded by a dark splotch.

Alice looked up at her, her eyes wide. "Uh-oh," she said. "What do you think it was? A snake?"

Rommy shook her head. "I don't know. My foot hit the bottom of the pool, and then there was all this pain. Maybe I hit something?"

"Do you think it was poisonous?" Alice frowned at the growing dark patch on Rommy's leg.

"I hope not," said Rommy. She gingerly stood up and put her foot on the cold stone floor. Pain streaked up her leg. She gave a one-legged hop and floated up into the air. "Good thing I can fly," she said, trying to smile around the pain.

"How do we get out of this place?" Alice asked, looking around. "I don't want to go out the way we came in, that's for sure."

"Finn said there was a tunnel that would lead us out to the far side of the cliffs," Rommy said.

"It's so dark in here. How are we supposed to find this tunnel without bashing our brains out on all those long things hanging from the ceiling?" Alice gestured at the stalagmites that hung at various lengths from the ceiling hiding in the darkness far above them.

Before Rommy could answer, a small light came whizzing at them. It made a tinkling sound as it did a loop around them.

"Ooh, it's Nissa," said Alice.

The fairy made a tighter circle around the girls and hovered in front of Rommy's leg. Her pant leg was still rolled up. The small creature made a hissing sound and then flew until she was eye level with Rommy. She started chittering and gesturing.

Rommy let out a sigh. "I'm sorry, but I don't know what you're saying," she said to the agitated fairy. The fairy spiraled down, and Rommy felt her lightly touching her leg. Suddenly, pain exploded up her leg, and Rommy sank to the hard stone ground. She thought she might be sick. After the initial burst of pain, her leg felt like someone had set it on fire. She tried to pull it away, but the fairy hissed and chittered at her again.

"What're you doing to her?" demanded Alice as she slid down next to Rommy.

Just when Rommy thought she couldn't bear the burning any longer, it simmered down to just warmth. The fairy rose again to flutter in front of Rommy's face. She clicked and whistled, gesturing with her tiny hands. Rommy still had no idea what she was saying.

"That splotchy spot is glowing now," reported Alice who was inspecting Rommy's leg.

Rommy looked at the tiny creature. Up close, she could see the fairy was wearing a silvery dress, and her hair was a pale lavender that matched her eyes. The fairy tinkled something at her and then buzzed away toward a distant spot in the cavern. Rommy tried to scramble up to follow, but her head whirled and she sank back down onto the ground.

"What's wrong with you?" Alice said.

"I...I don't know, but I feel strange," said Rommy. The cavern seemed to be spinning around her, and no matter where she looked, nothing would stay still. Blackness crowded at the corners of her vision.

The last thing Rommy saw was Alice's worried face and a tiny silvery light.

Chapter 13:
Alice Spills the Beans

As Rommy swam up out of the darkness, she could hear voices murmuring. She tried to focus, to identify who was speaking and what they were saying, but all she could make out were snatches of conversation.

"... brought her...fast..."

"Wot's wrong...breathing all funny..."

Rommy felt heat on her leg again. It kept getting hotter, and she struggled to pull her leg away, but a strong hand held her limb in place. Something cool and wet pushed against her lips, and she swallowed.

The voices faded away again, and she sank back into the blackness.

ROMMY BECAME AWARE of voices. Softness covered her. She cracked her eyes open and blinked. A wizened face came into view.

"Welcome back," said a soothing voice, and the wrinkled face broke into a smile. A gentle hand smoothed back her hair.

She tried to speak, but her mouth was so dry, all she did was croak. A cup appeared, and cool water flowed between her lips.

She sputtered and then swallowed. "Where am I? What happened?" She struggled to sit up, but gentle hands pressed her back down onto the bed.

"Gently, gently," said the old woman who was tending her. "You're here in my home."

Two more heads popped into view, one small with big violet eyes and the other with shaggy dark hair and gray eyes that weren't laughing at the moment.

"You're alive!" said Alice. "I thought you were a goner, for sure. If it hadn't a been for Finn, here, you woulda been, too." Alice jerked her thumb at the boy who stood next to her, his face grim.

Rommy blinked her eyes, trying to remember what had happened. The memories came rushing back—diving into the pool, being pushed down by the pounding water, the searing pain in her leg.

Her eyes widened in sudden understanding. "Something bit me! Is that what's wrong with me? Was it poisonous?" She looked from the elderly woman to Finn and back to Alice.

Little Owl's face was gentle as she answered. "You were bitten by a singing eel. They generally don't bother people, but you must have disturbed one. They seem to be poisonous only to a few, and you, Child, are one of them. Usually a singing eel bite just makes you feel poorly for a day or two, but for some people, it brings a worse illness and even death. You are lucky that young Finn brought you here so quickly."

"Brought me here?" Rommy looked from Little Owl to Finn, who was avoiding her gaze and staring at his feet. "Do you mean you carried me all the way here?" She could feel a blush working its way up her neck.

"I didn't have much choice," said Finn, shrugging his shoulders. "It was bring you here to Little Owl or let you die."

"Your face turned this awful color," said Alice, shoving closer to Rommy. "It was this blueish purple color, and you made these gurgling noises. I thought you was a croaker for sure."

"How did you...I mean how am I okay?" Rommy asked, looking at Little Owl.

"Between the magical folk and a special plant that grows on the far side of the island, I can heal the ones who get here in time," said Little Owl.

Rommy glanced around. Then her eyes widened, and she clutched at Finn's arm. "Does Pan know you are here?" she asked.

Finn shrugged. "I don't think so." Then he grinned. "Last time I saw him, he was hightailing it out of there with a dozen night parrots after him."

"Were those the things that came flying down?" said Rommy. "All I saw were lots of bright feathers."

Finn nodded, satisfaction on his face. "They aren't Pan's biggest fans. He steals their feathers, and night parrots have long memories."

Rommy grinned up at Finn but then sobered. "Won't he suspect you helped us? Shouldn't you get back already?"

Finn waved a hand. "Nah, he's probably on the other side of the island by now, holed up somewhere. He usually sleeps until midmorning, anyway. It's not quite dawn, so I've got plenty of time."

"Dawn?" Rommy pushed herself up to sitting and tried to swing her legs over the side of the narrow bed.

Little Owl blocked her progress. "You cannot leave yet. You must rest a while more. I removed the poison from your leg, but it has made you weak. You aren't out of danger just yet."

"But my father..." said Rommy. "He doesn't know I'm gone. He'll be so upset."

"We will send word to your father," said Little Owl.

Rommy was thankful Little Owl didn't ask why her father was unaware she had left his ship in the middle of the night. Now she had a different problem, and that was how to get back aboard without Papa knowing she'd been gone. She glanced over at Alice. Of course, she'd have to come up with a reason the little girl had turned up, but Rommy was sure she could come up with something.

"It would be best if we returned to the ship before my father...well, before he realizes I'm not there," she said.

Little Owl looked at her but said nothing. Rommy could feel the heat climbing up her neck again, and she looked away from the piercing black eyes. Did Little Owl know what Tiger Lily had done? She had to, since Alice had gone missing. Rommy swung her gaze back to Little Owl's and lifted her chin.

"We, that is, Finn and I, were rescuing Alice," said Rommy. "My father, well, when he's around Peter Pan, he loses focus. I needed to get Alice to a safe place and away from Pan."

Rommy watched sorrow come over Little Owl's face. "You have kindly not mentioned the part my granddaughter played in the need for Alice's rescue." She gently placed a hand on Rommy's cheek. "You have a kind heart for so fierce a warrior."

Rommy dropped her eyes, unable to bear the sadness in the old woman's face.

"Young Tiger Lily's heart is not her own anymore, and it makes her do foolish things," said Little Owl with a deep sigh, shaking her head. "Her father has confined her to her sleeping place. We have always aligned ourselves with Pan over your father for the sake of the little ones, but Pan has shown that he is not to be completely trusted."

"You ain't kidding!" said Alice, settling on the bed next to Rommy. "Half those Lost Boys was stolen—right out of their beds. Poor Jem is so nervy, he jumps at every little noise."

Little Owl turned the young girl to face her. "What are you saying? Is this true? Peter Pan has been stealing children?"

Alice nodded her head and then shrugged. "Wellll, not all of them. Oscar and Willie and a few of the others was street boys who didn't have nothing better to do than to come here. I mean, at least they eat kinda regular now."

Little Owl pulled the little girl closer. "How many?"

Alice looked at her hands and counted on her fingers. "I didn't ask for no show of hands or nothing, but I'd say maybe..." she looked down at her fingers again. "Maybe four of 'em."

Little Owl rose surprisingly quickly from beside the bed. "I must speak to my son about this." She started toward the entrance before turning back at Rommy. "I will send Little Bear to get word to your father. You mustn't try to leave before then." Seeing the alarm on Rommy's face, she smiled. "Your father may bellow, but remember, the louder he is the more his heart cares."

Rommy sank back on the pillow. She didn't look forward to hearing how much her father's heart cared.

Chapter 14:
A New Quest

Rommy looked at Alice. "Are you sure that Pan stole those boys?"

Alice rolled her eyes. "Do you think I'm thick in the head? Course I know."

Rommy looked over at Finn, whose face was curiously blank.

"Did you know about this?" Rommy asked.

Finn looked away from her and shrugged. "I guess," he said.

"You guess? How long has this been going on? Did Pan kidnap you, too?" She leaned forward to get a glimpse of his face. He was now looking around at the insides of Little Owl's curious conical home.

"No, he didn't steal me," said Finn, jutting out his chin. "I came with him 'cause I wanted to. Both my parents was dead, and the rich toffs my mum worked for thought I'd make a nice punching bag once she was gone. Peter seemed like the better lot at the time."

Rommy's face softened. "I'm sorry," she said, putting a hand on his arm. He shrugged it off.

"It was a long time ago," he said. "I hardly remember either of them. It doesn't matter."

"It does matter," Rommy said, leaning toward him and covering his clenched fist with her hand. Her hazel eyes met his gray ones. "Nobody should be treated like that. Nobody." Finn just stared at Rommy. She couldn't seem to look away.

"What's with you two?" Alice said, looking between the two.

Rommy snatched her hand back, and her face felt uncomfortably warm. She cleared her throat.

"When did Pan start taking children, Finn? Do you know?"

Finn shrugged again. "I'm not sure. I told you time isn't the same in Neverland. But it was a while ago. Maybe half of the boys isn't here because they chose it, though."

Rommy remembered Sebastian and the child that said a flying boy had pulled him into the bushes. It seemed like Pan stole her brother, too.

"How many Lost Boys have there been? Why haven't you stopped Pan from taking children?"

"Peter isn't someone you cross, Rommy," said Finn, sitting on the foot of the bed.

"I would think you'd cross him for something like this, Finn. I didn't take you for a coward," said Rommy, clenching her fists.

Finn pushed up from the bed in one fluid movement and loomed over Rommy. "You think you know so much after only a few days in Neverland, do you? Shoulda known a girl like you wouldn't understand what it's really like here." Finn spun away from her.

"A girl like me?" Rommy said. "What's that supposed to mean, anyway? How am I supposed to understand if nobody will tell me anything?"

Finn kept his back to her. "You don't understand what Pan is capable of or how dangerous he really is. The only way I can protect the Lost Boys is to stay with them. If I cross Pan, do you think he'd just let it go? If I was lucky, I'd be exiled." Finn blew out a breath. "Not all the Lost Boys die in battles with your father, you know."

Rommy sank back against the pillow and swallowed. "I'm...I'm sorry, Finn. I didn't mean to imply...that is...how many of them have...died?" The last word came out in a whisper.

Finn crossed his arms. "Not as many as would have if I didn't look out for them. I tell them how to stay on Pan's good side." His gaze narrowed. "That father of yours doesn't help matters, either."

"My father? He doesn't seem to be the real problem here," said Rommy.

"He is not the problem I thought he was," said Chief Hawk Eye who had opened the entrance flap and was standing with Little Owl.

Rommy looked up with a start and then smiled at the solemn man. He returned her smile, making him appear less intimidating.

"I am sorry to see you taken ill," he said, nodding at Rommy.

"Little Owl has taken good care of me, and I'm feeling much better," said Rommy.

Seemingly done with the pleasantries, Chief Hawk Eye turned his dark eyes on Alice. "Little Owl has told me the disturbing news. Is it true, little one, that Peter Pan has been stealing children? Are you quite sure?"

Alice threw up her hands and snorted. "What is it with you people? When a kid says, 'I was sleeping and then someone was flying away with me,' it's not hard to chivvy out his meaning."

A smile quirked one corner of Chief Hawk Eye's mouth, and he inclined his head in Alice's direction. "My apologies for doubting your word."

Alice crossed her arms and nodded.

Chief Hawk Eye's smile melted away as he looked at Finn. "Has Pan told you why he does this?"

Finn stuck his hands in his pockets. "No, but then, who knows why Pan does anything. He's gotten worse since I came here. Used to be, you could talk a bit of sense to him, but now, he gets angrier than a load of jackers if you kicked their nest." Finn paused and looked up from his study of the floor. "You don't dare cross Pan, if you know what's good for you."

Chief Hawk Eye frowned and turned toward Little Owl. "Mother, what is to be done here? You have been here longer than any of us."

Little Owl walked toward the center of her home, a troubled look on her face. "The passage between Neverland and the outside world has not always been open."

Chief Hawk Eye gave his mother a startled glance. "It hasn't?"

Little Owl gave a gentle smile. "No, it hasn't. It was opened during my grandmother's time, and Peter appeared shortly after our people crossed over to this place. One fairy, Tinkerbell, I think it was, pleaded that he be allowed to come here."

"But why?" asked Rommy, now sitting straight up on the bed.

Little Owl took a seat in a willow rocking chair near the bed. "The only ones who know that are Tinkerbell, Peter Pan, and Unilisi."

"Oo Na who-ey?" asked Alice, wrinkling her nose.

Little Owl chuckled. "It is said Oo-Na-Lee-See. It means grandmother of many. She is the Life Tree in the center of this island. She is the source of all its magic, and she controlled the passageway between this island and the world from which you came."

Alice's eyes got wide, and she stared first at Little Owl and then at Rommy. "This is like some kind of fairy tale or something."

"You said 'controlled,'" said Rommy. "Doesn't she control that passageway anymore?"

Little Owl smiled. "How clever you are to hear that," she said. "I only know what my grandmother told me, and that was many moons ago now. But, there was a way to open the passageway that only Unilisi knew. Now that it is open, I believe there is a way that would close it again, but I don't know what that way is. I don't even know if Unilisi would bother herself to get involved enough to close the passage again, unless there was a very good reason. You would have to seek her out to find the answer to that question."

Rommy threw back the blanket and tried to swing her legs over the side of the bed. "Then we need to go find her and ask."

Before she could stand up, Little Owl put a hand on her shoulder.

"Slow down, Child," she said as she gently pushed Rommy's legs back onto the bed. "You are not well enough to go anywhere at the moment, and I'm sure your father would be most unhappy if you went missing again, would he not?"

Rommy felt her face color under the older woman's scrutiny, but she lifted her chin. "Someone has to stop Pan. I was hoping to get Papa to go back to London, to forget about Pan, but..." she looked down at her hands which were tightly clasped in her lap, "...after hearing this, we can't just leave, even if I could persuade Papa." She looked up into Little Owl's eyes again. "It would be wrong. We have to go to this Unilisi and get her to close that passage. It's the only way now."

Little Owl placed a hand on Rommy's head. "You have a noble heart, Child, but Unilisi resides in the middle of the jungle. The journey is very dangerous with no guarantee of success. Unilisi is not like you or I. She is an ancient being, and she does not always take kindly to those who disturb her. Even if she allowed you to approach her, she might refuse to answer your questions."

"You mean this here tree lady might just tell us to go away after we go all that way to see her? She doesn't sound so great to me," said Alice.

"We have to take that chance," said Rommy. "We can't just leave Pan to plunder people."

Little Owl smiled at the little girl and then looked at Rommy. "You must think long and hard about making this journey. It will not be easy, and it might all be for nothing in the end."

Rommy clenched her fists. "I will make this Unilisi see how important this is," she said fiercely. "If she has any conscience at all, she won't want children brought here against their will."

Chief Hawk Eye stepped forward. "What you say has merit, but my mother is right. You cannot make this trip alone."

"She ain't going alone," interrupted Alice. "I aim to go with her."

Chief Hawk Eye let out a bark of laughter. "I have no doubt, little one, but even as strong as you are, Captain Hook's daughter will need more help than just you." He turned back toward Rommy. "You cannot go now, though. You must return with your father and rest and get well. I have sent Little Bear with a message for him, and he should collect you soon."

Rommy flopped back against the pillow and groaned. "Papa will be so angry with me," she said, putting her hand over her face.

Little Owl chuckled.

"Your father and my people have not been friends, but we have both refrained from outright attacking each other," Chief Hawk Eye said and then paused.

Rommy lowered her hands and looked up at the tall man. His face was stern as he stared down at her before continuing. "It is important that nothing happens to you while you are under our care. If you want to make this journey, we cannot help you. Do you understand what I am telling you?"

Rommy sighed. Part of her understood Chief Hawk Eye's position, but another part of her wished all the adults could put aside their differences for something as important as children being kidnapped. She nodded at him. He gave a slight smile, and his face lost its tense expression.

"I will leave you to rest now until Captain Hook comes for you," he said nodding at them. "Come, Mother." The two of them walked toward the entrance, ducked through the flap, and were gone.

Chapter 15: Rommy's Turn to Spill the Beans

Rommy looked at Alice and Finn. "You realize we have to go find this Unilisi and get her to tell us how to close that passageway, right? I know we can't go now, even if I were completely well. It would cause problems for the Chief and Little Owl."

"I wouldn't mind seeing some trouble for that Tiger Lily, though," said Alice scowling.

Rommy quirked an eyebrow. "You and me both, but she's not our biggest concern right now."

Finn held up a hand. "How do you propose to go all the way to the center of the jungle without some help? I know you think you can do anything, but Little Owl wasn't lying when she said it was dangerous. If one of the animals don't kill you, some plant will."

"It can't be that bad. There has to be a way," said Rommy, and then she gave Finn her most charming smile. "Maybe you can help me."

Finn snorted. "Oh yes, I'll just tell Pan I need a bit of time off to go on a little trip." He rolled his eyes. "That shouldn't get his suspicions up or anything!"

Rommy dropped the smile and hit her fist on the blanket. "I have to get to that tree. Someone has to stop Pan!"

"You don't have to tell me, but what do you want me to do about it? If Pan thinks I'm trying to double-cross him, my life won't be worth a zippet." Finn kicked at a ball of yarn lying near the rocking chair, sending it spinning across the room. "Why don't you ask that father of yours to help you?"

It was Rommy's turn to roll her eyes. "He's so protective of me, he'd send me away first," she said. "I can't let him do that. Besides, he has so many enemies on this island, Unilisi probably wouldn't tell him anything."

"And whose fault is that? He hasn't exactly been Mr. Friendly since he just showed up here out of the blue. I mean, one of the first things he did was kill off old Captain One-Eyed Willy. Then he took over his crew and made it his mission to get Pan. I don't even understand how he got here." Finn paused and gave her a hard look. "But some of the fairies tell nasty stories of how he stole their pixie dust for that ship of his."

Rommy leaned forward and pointed her finger at him. "You're not helping, Finn," she said. "You make a big show about being all concerned about the Lost Boys, but when we have a way to help them, all you do is tell me how I can't go into the jungle and how you can't help me and all the other things that can't be done. Why won't you be helpful for a change?"

"Me not being helpful? What about your old man? He just makes everything worse. I know you think he's so wonderful, but all he does is make things harder. Why is he even here?"

Rommy looked away and bit her lip.

"Oh, that's right. Your oh-so-perfect father doesn't tell you anything, does he? Things like he's a pirate or why he came to Neverland, anyway." Finn curled his lip.

Rommy narrowed her eyes. "That's all you know. Papa *did* tell me why he's here and why he wants revenge so badly, but if you assume I'm telling you..." she crossed her arms.

"Never mind about him," said Alice, shoving Finn to the side. "Tell *me*!" The little girl leaned in close, her eyes huge in her face.

Finn leaned back against the pole that went up through the middle of Little Owl's home. "Yeah, why don't you tell both of us, if it's such a good reason."

Rommy looked at both of them, Alice'd eyes wide with curiosity and Finn looking bored. She blew out a breath. "My brother was a Lost Boy," she said. "Pan nabbed him while Papa and Mama were picnicking in the park. He was only 5. Before Papa could find him, my brother was killed fighting your One-Eyed Willy. My mama died, too—from the shock of my brother's disappearance, according to my father."

Finn stared at her, his mouth slightly ajar.

"Blimey! No wonder your old man hates Pan so much!" said Alice.

Finn shoved his hands into his pockets. "What was his name?" he asked.

"What?"

"His name—what was it?"

"Sebastian," said Rommy. "His name was Sebastian."

Finn snapped his fingers and pointed at her. "I knew a Sebastian. He arrived not long after I did. There was a big battle with old One-Eyed Willy. He was a brave little chap." Finn coughed and rubbed the back of his neck. "I reckon Captain Hook has reason enough to hate Pan. I guess he ain't as bad as I thought."

Light suddenly slanted in as the flap to the dwelling opened. "You don't know how relieved I am to hear your elevated opinion of me," drawled a familiar voice.

Chapter 16:
Papa's Anger

"Papa!" Rommy gasped as Finn looked around wildly for another exit.

Her father stopped Finn with a piercing stare. He stepped to the side of the doorway and pointed his hook at the boy. "Get out," he said in a menacing voice. "Get out and don't ever come near my daughter again, or you will be sorry."

Rommy saw Finn swallow, but he didn't move toward the entrance. "I...I want to be sure she'll be okay, sir—before I leave, that is," he said. He looked over at Rommy who was staring at him, her mouth ajar.

Hook gave a bark of laughter, but the sound made a ripple of dismay go up Rommy's spine. "Your devotion is nothing short of alarming," he said, and walked to where Finn stood. "However, she wouldn't need your tender concern if you hadn't brought her here in the first place." His voice came out in a bellow, his breath making Finn's hair blow backward. Hook closed his eyes briefly and straightened. Drawing a deep breath, he exhaled slowly.

Then he continued in a softer voice. "But, as I understand it, your bringing her to Little Owl probably saved her life, so I'll let you leave here in one piece. However," Hook leaned forward and thumped the end of his hook on Finn's chest, "if I catch you in her vicinity again, I won't be quite so understanding, boy."

Finn didn't shrink back, but his clenched fists shook a little.

Hook straightened and stared down his long nose at Finn. "Now," he said, enunciating each word, "get out." Hook pulled open the flap to the tent and gestured. Finn gave Rommy one last glance, and then, with his head up, he walked out.

Hook swung his gaze to Rommy. She shrank back from the anger in his eyes. "And you," he pointed his hook at her, but he seemed too angry to even speak. He closed his eyes, and his nostrils flared as he took several deep breaths before opening his eyes again. It didn't seem to help all that much.

In two strides he was by her bedside and had grasped her arm. He shook it, and she hissed as his fingers closed over the new wound Pan had given her. Seeing her response seemed only to fuel his rage. "You're hurt? Again?" he all but shouted.

Rommy tried to pull away from him. This was a Papa she didn't know, with his blazing eyes and teeth bared in a snarl. She stared at him mutely. She couldn't help the tears that welled in her eyes.

Instead of softening him, though, her tears only seemed to make her father angrier, which she hadn't thought was possible. "Enough of that, do you hear me?" he shook her arm again. "I won't be pulled in by those crocodile tears again. I've been entirely too soft with you."

"Stop it, Papa! You're hurting me," she said. Her arm was now throbbing where his fingers dug into the cut.

He gritted his teeth. "You're lucky I don't do worse, young lady. How could you be so foolish as to present yourself to Pan like some kind of gift? Do you realize what he could have done to you?"

"I ain't seeing that you're much better," came a small voice. Rommy and Hook both turned to see Alice standing there, her arms crossed and a ferocious scowl on her face. She turned to Rommy.

"This your old man you keep telling me about?" She looked Hook up and down, and the look of contempt she gave him wasn't one that belonged on a six-year-old's face. "He don't seem all that wonderful to me."

Hook dropped Rommy's arm and stared down at the little girl. "And who are you?"

"I'm Alice, and you've gotta be Captain Hook, Rommy's old man." She shook her head and looked at Rommy. "How did you not know he was a pirate?"

Rommy took in her father's flowing black hair, the gold hoop winking in his ear, and the dagger strapped to his waist and realized Alice was right. Her father not only looked like a pirate, but at the moment, he was acting like one, too. Papa had always been larger than life when he'd swoop in on his visits, but standing in the dim light, he seemed dangerous. Rommy blinked away her tears and took a deep breath. She knew Papa would be angry with her. Now, she just had to deal with it.

She swung her legs over the side of the bed, and Hook whirled around to face her again. "And where do you think you're going?"

Rommy pushed to her feet. The room swayed, but she stiffened her knees. She lifted her chin, and there was an edge to her voice now. "I'm getting ready to leave, Papa. That's why you came, isn't it? To take me back to the ship?"

"Do not speak to me in that tone, Andromeda," Hook said, looming over her. Rommy forced herself not to step back. She felt her own anger flickering to life. "You are fortunate I don't turn you over my knee right here and give you the thrashing you so clearly need. Of all the harebrained schemes..." He punctuated his words with his hook.

"Well, her schemes sure helped me out, harebrained or not," said Alice. "Being stuck with Pan was no picnic, and you jolly well made sticks and stones the first time around, didn't you?"

Hook spun to stare down his nose at the small girl frowning up at him. He lifted both brows. "I'm not sure why you would think I care a tuppence how you feel, little miss, but I'll thank you to keep those thoughts to yourself. This is between my daughter and me." He curled his lip. "You are fortunate I'm willing to take on a little baggage like you."

Alice snorted. "Bag of wind, you are!"

"Why you..."

Rommy latched onto her father's arm. "What is wrong with you, Papa? Why are you acting like this? I'm sorry I worried you, but I didn't have a choice."

"No choice? No choice?" Hook was bellowing again. "Do you know how it felt to have Little Bear tell me my daughter had almost died? I didn't even know you were gone!" Hook's voice cracked on the word gone, and guilt washed over Rommy at the anguish on her father's face.

"Oh, Papa, I am sorry. Truly, but Pan sent a note. He said if I didn't come, he'd hurt Alice. I had to go, and I couldn't..." She stopped and bit her lip.

"You couldn't what, Andromeda?"

Rommy looked away from her father and said nothing.

"Answer me," he said.

"I couldn't trust you not to go after Pan again, Papa," she said finally in a small voice. "I couldn't...I couldn't risk Alice getting hurt."

Hook stared at her for a long moment. "I see," he said, his tone flat.

In one swift motion, he scooped her up in his arms.

Rommy squirmed. "I'm fine, Papa," she said. "It's not too far. I can walk."

He squeezed her until she was still. "It's for me to say what you can and cannot do." Looking back at Alice, he said, "I'm assuming you can keep up then?"

"I ain't the one you oughta be worrying about," said Alice.

"We shouldn't impose on Chief Hawk Eye's hospitality any longer," he said. He strode toward the entrance, and Alice scrambled after him.

Rommy opened her mouth to protest but her father gave her a hard look. "This conversation is not over, Andromeda, but we will finish it on the ship. If you know what is good for you, I'd advise you to be silent."

Rommy snapped her mouth shut, but her mind was whirring.

As he carried her out of the tent, they were met by Chief Hawk Eye, Little Owl, and Little Bear. Without ceremony, Hook turned and dumped her into the arms of Big Red who was standing close by with Gentleman Jack. Rommy's cheeks heated. She was embarrassed at being hauled out of the camp like a bag of flour. Gentleman Jack caught her eye and winked.

Her father seemed to expand as he turned back to Chief Hawk Eye. He gave a small, formal bow.

"You have my thanks, Chief Hawk Eye, for your excellent care of my daughter." He turned and inclined his head toward Little Owl. "And you have my deepest gratitude for saving her life. I am in your debt."

Chief Hawk Eye's face was inscrutable as he looked at Hook for a long moment before replying. "Your daughter is welcome here. She is a noble girl with a good and true heart."

Rommy noticed the Chief said nothing about her Papa's heart. Of course, her father had tied Tiger Lily to the rock in Mermaid Lagoon. He made everyone think he would let her drown if she didn't tell him where Pan was. It would be unlikely that Chief Hawk Eye and her father would be friends after all that. Still, she was relieved the two seemed to have called a truce of sorts.

Rommy looked across at the Little Owl. The older woman met her eyes and walked to where Big Red was standing. She put a gnarled hand on Rommy's and squeezed it.

Rommy smiled at the older woman. "Thank you," she said. "I owe you my life."

"I am always here to help, Child. All you need to do is ask." Then the older woman gave a smile and wink.

Chief Hawk Eye came to stand next to his mother. He put a hand on Rommy's shoulder. "May you wake healthy and go forward with courage," he said in a kind of benediction. His mouth curved in a slight smile before he stepped back.

Alice had no such reservations. She hugged first LIttle Owl, then Little Bear and finally Chief Hawk Eye. He gently tousled her dark brown curls. "Go safely, little one."

Hook made an impatient gesture. "Come along," he said. "We mustn't impose any longer." He nodded again at the chief and turned away, striding down the path away from the encampment.

Big Red followed with Rommy in his arms. Alice trotted next to him and Gentleman Jack brought up the rear. A heavy silence fell over the group as they walked up the path. Rommy wasn't looking forward to the conversation that was sure to happen once she got back to the ship.

Chapter 17:
Papa's Threat

When the little party finally reached the shore, Big Red set Rommy gently into the rowboat next to her father. He didn't acknowledge her presence. Alice, her face rather pinched, sat crowded against Rommy. Big Red and Gentleman Jack pushed the boat out into the water and then jumped in after, making the boat bob wildly from side to side.

Rommy took in Alice's white face and the death grip she had on the seat and put her arm around the younger girl. "We'll be fine," she whispered in Alice's ear, but Alice didn't seem reassured. Her body remained tense as the two crewmen rowed them out to the big ship.

When they reached the side of the ship, a rope ladder was slung over the side. Alice shook her head. "I ain't getting on that thing. No way, no how!" she said.

Rommy squeezed Alice's hand. "You don't have to," she said. "You can just fly." Alice pushed off into the air, but before Rommy could follow, her father grasped her around the waist and slung her over his shoulder.

Her face burned by the time her father made it to the deck railing and climbed over with her hanging upside down. He set her down on the deck with a thud that reverberated through her injured leg and made it throb. Rommy wished a large hole would form in the deck when she saw the dozen staring eyes. Alice sidled up to her and stood close.

Her father looked around at the men. "What are you looking at?" he barked. "Get back to work!" Turning to Rommy, he said in that same flat voice, "Show Alice to your cabin, and then I want you to wait for me in mine."

Without even waiting to see if Rommy would follow his directions, he strode off across the deck, shouting orders, and scattering men as he went.

Her father's expression sent prickles of alarm up Rommy's spine. Her father usually blustered and bellowed, but this was different. Without a word, she led Alice to her cabin and opened the door.

"You should probably stay in here," said Rommy.

Alice looked at her with worried eyes. "Your old man ain't gonna beat you, is he?"

Rommy swallowed. "He's never lifted a hand to me in my entire life."

"Well, he didn't have no problem grabbing your arm and about rattling your teeth out of your head."

Rommy straightened her shoulders. "He was just upset and not acting himself. He would never truly hurt me."

Alice grabbed her hand. "I'm sorry. You're in all this trouble because of me."

Rommy smiled down at Alice and squeezed her hand. "Alice, this isn't your fault. It's Pan's fault. He's the reason Papa is here. He's the one who took you, and it certainly isn't your fault that my father has a terrible temper."

Alice wrapped her small arms around Rommy's waist. Rommy hugged her back and then gently pushed her away.

"I'll be fine, Alice," she said as she moved confidently toward the door.

"Good luck!" said Alice as Rommy shut the door behind her.

Out of Alice's sight, Rommy's shoulders sagged. She wasn't nearly as sure of things as she had wanted Alice to believe. Her father's angry face kept looming up in her mind, and her arm still hurt from where he'd grabbed her.

She walked into her father's cabin on wooden legs and took a seat on a chair by the table. The minutes ticked by and with each moment that passed, her dread grew. Her imagination supplied all kinds of terrible possibilities. When the door finally opened, it was almost a relief. She shot to her feet and faced her father.

He came into the cabin and shut the door behind him with exaggerated care. He folded his arms across his barrel-like chest and stared at her long and hard without saying a word. She would rather he bellow at her. At least then, she knew how to react. His long stare was unnerving her.

"Papa, I..." she began, unable to take the leaden silence a moment longer.

Her father held up his hand to stop her. "I brought you in here to tell you we are leaving. As soon as I can get the ship ready, we will pull out to return to London." She opened her mouth, but he continued talking. "No, don't say a word. Not. One. Word." He bit off each syllable with a dangerous calmness. "You've made it clear that you don't trust me, and because of that, I can't trust you not to pull another stunt like you did tonight. I cannot constantly worry about something happen-ing to you. I should have sent you back immediately, but fool that I am, I succumbed to weak emotions, wanting you here with me." He paused and drew in a deep breath.

"Papa, I want..."

Her father crossed the room and before she could blink, had her chin in an almost painful grip. He leaned down until they were almost nose-to-nose. "I don't want to hear it," he said through gritted teeth. "You are my daughter, and I said we are leaving. We will return to London, and you and your lit-tle friend Alice will stay at the townhouse until I find another place for you. I'll leave Big Red with you for protection, and that is the end of this discussion. You may go to your cabin and stay there until we are under way."

"But Papa," she said, pleading, "I can't leave. You don't un-derstand. Pan is stealing children just like he did with Sebast-ian. We're the only ones that can stop him. Don't you see?"

Her father straightened. "*We* don't have to do anything. I will take care of Pan—after you return to London."

Rommy grabbed his arm. "But I can help you," she said.

Her father stared down at her and shook his head. "You could have so easily died today, Andromeda," he said, his voice catching. "I will not lose you, too. I won't."

"I won't stay," she said desperately. "Once we get to Lon-don, I'll find a way to come back."

Her father narrowed his eyes as he pulled his arm away from her grasp. "Do you or don't you want Alice to come along with you? She doesn't have to, you know. I'm sure Little Owl would be happy to take her back." His lip curled. "She'd still be better off than where she came from." He straightened his cuffs. "I suppose you'll have to hope Tiger Lily won't make another kidnapping attempt."

Rommy stared at him. "You don't mean that!"

"I think you know that I do," he said, stepping away from her. "Don't make me be the villain because I assure you, I can be." He gave a thin-lipped smile. "I've gotten used to it."

He walked to the door and put his hand on the doorknob. For a moment, he looked back at her, his face twisting, and then, whirling, he was gone.

"Oh Papa," said Rommy softly, "I'm afraid you already are." Slowly, she walked toward the door. She had to leave Neverland. Pan would continue to steal children. Her father would continue to chase him for who knew how long. He might die. And there was nothing she could do about it. A sob wrenched out of her as she opened the door.

Chapter 18:
It's Hopeless

Rommy hurried toward her own cabin, tucking her chin down so none of the men scurrying around the deck would see the tears that were falling fast and thick. When she opened the door, Alice let out a squawk of alarm.

"What happened?" Alice asked, rushing toward Rommy.

Rommy threw herself onto the bed as sobs shook her. "He...he's...taking...us back...to...London," she got out before burying her face deeper into the pillow.

Alice sat on the side of the bed and patted Rommy's back. "It'll be okay," she said. "You'll talk him round."

Rommy shook her head. "Not...not this...time."

Alice continued to sit with Rommy, trying to convince her that everything would be okay, but Rommy knew better. Finally, she wiped at her face and sat up, her shoulders slumping.

"You'll convince him to let ya stay," said Alice, shoving a handkerchief into Rommy's hand who mopped at her face.

Rommy shook her head. "Not this time," she said. "Oh Alice, if I don't go, he'll...he'll keep you here."

Alice blinked at her. "You really had no idea your old man was a pirate? I don't know how you missed that one."

Rommy just looked at Alice. "He isn't acting like himself. He was never like this before."

"But you never saw him much, did you?" Alice asked and shrugged. "Maybe this *is* what he's really like, and what you *remember* was him not acting like himself."

Rommy hugged her pillow to her chest. "I'm not sure I like this Papa very much."

Alice plopped down on the bed and slung her arm around Rommy's shoulders. "He's got a temper, that's for sure, but nobody could be as wonderful as the papa you carry around in your noggin. Nobody's that good."

"Perhaps you're right." Rommy threw the pillow aside and stood up. "But that doesn't change the fact that he's taking us back to London. I'll be right back where I started—waiting around and worrying about my father. Not to mention Pan will be skipping around London, plucking children from their beds."

Alice stood, too. "Why do you hafta go back to London?"

"Didn't you understand what I said?" Rommy said and immediately regretted her sharp tone.

"Yeah, I got you, but people telling you no ain't never stopped you afore. Why are you giving up so easy this time?"

"But Papa will keep you here, and he might even take you back to Little Owl," protested Rommy. "What if Tiger Lily tries something else?"

Alice waved a hand. "I ain't afraid of her. She only got the better of me 'cause she surprised me." Alice scowled. "She won't be doing that again."

"But still if we get caught, Papa will make good on his promise," Rommy said. "If you'd seen his face, you'd know he means every word."

Alice grinned up at her. "I don't need to see his face because we ain't gonna to get caught." Alice nudged Rommy with her elbow. "Besides, if your old man thinks I'm going to just do what he says, he's balmy on the crumpet."

A smile tugged at Rommy's mouth, but she was silent for a long moment. Finally, she looked at Alice. "You're really willing to risk it?"

Alice shrugged. "We've come this far. It seems an awful shame to give up now."

Slowly an answering grin spread across Rommy's face. "You're right! I don't know why I let it all seem so impossible. "

Alice rolled her eyes. "I've been wondering that ever since you come in here caterwauling."

Rommy ignored the comment. "I think Little Owl will help us. At least she seemed to indicate that when we left."

Alice clapped her hands. "Now, that's more like it. Do you have a plan?"

The two girls sat back down on the bed. "The timing is important," said Rommy. "We can't let Papa find out we're gone until after he's left the island. We'll have to sneak off at the very last moment. Hopefully, by the time he discovers we aren't on the ship, he'll be so far away it will take ages for him to get back. By then, maybe we'll know how to close that passage, and we can all go home."

Chapter 19:
Good-bye, Papa

Rommy and Alice spent the morning making plans. The biggest problem was not knowing when her father would pull anchor and leave. As she explained to Alice, the more time passed before Papa realized they were gone, the better.

Alice was rolling up their clothes when the door swung open. Both girls plopped down on the bed to hide their packing.

Smee came bustling into the room, holding a tray piled high with food. "Well now, the Captain has relented at last and said I could feed you two darling girls," he said, looking around for a place to put the tray.

Rommy could see him eyeing the bed. "Why don't you put it over there, Mr. Smee?" she said, gesturing toward the chair by the little stove. "It will stay warmer over there."

Smee gingerly balanced it on the seat and turned back to the two girls. His dark eyes alighted on Alice, and he raised his bushy gray eyebrows in Rommy's direction.

Rommy stood up and made the introductions. Smee came over and took the hand Alice offered him, squeezing it between his plump ones. "We are so glad to have you on board, my dear girl. Any friend of Rommy's is a friend of ours. You make yourself right at home," he said.

"You sure don't look like any pirate I've ever seen," said Alice, looking the small, round man up and down.

Smee beamed at her and patted her head. "Aren't you a sweet little thing?"

"Ain't nobody called me sweet before, neither," said Alice, pulling away from the patting hand.

Smee chuckled.

"Mr. Smee, Papa said we were leaving," said Rommy. "Do you know when that will be? I'd love to see us pull up anchor. It would be so exciting." She smiled sweetly at Smee. "Does it take long to sail to London?"

He patted her cheek. "Why, my darling girl, we won't be sailing to London. That would take too long."

"We won't?" Rommy opened her eyes wide. "How in the world will we be getting there?" She stepped on Alice's foot because the younger girl was rolling her eyes.

"Why, we'll be flying, of course," said Smee. He clapped his hands together. "I expect Big Red is pulling anchor as we speak, and trust me, when we leave the water, you'll know it." He smiled and winked at her. "It's certainly quite an experience."

"I'd love to go out on deck and watch," said Rommy.

Smee frowned. "Poor lamb, I don't assume the Captain will cotton to that idea at the moment. He wants you to stay in here." Smee glanced at Alice. "Both of you, that is."

Rommy made a show of being disappointed but resigned. "Oh, well, if that is what Papa wants, I suppose we must stay in here, then."

Smee patted her hand. "There's a good girl, but don't you worry. Once we're aloft, I'm sure the Captain will let you come out on deck. It is quite thrilling to be sailing through nothing but thin air."

With a last smile at the girls, Smee turned toward the door, calling over his shoulder, "Don't you worry. It will be a wonderful trip. You wait and see."

The door clicked behind him. Rommy gestured to Alice. "Hurry and put those clothes in this sack," she said, handing the younger girl a rough sack that she had found underneath the bed. "I'll get the food." She placed the bread, smoked fish, and pieces of fruit in the napkins Smee had provided.

Rommy pulled a few other items out of the trunk at the foot of the bed and handed them to Alice. She wished there was a way to get into her father's cabin and get some kind of weapon. Traveling anywhere in Neverland, never mind the jungle, without something to protect herself made her shudder. She squared her shoulders. She couldn't dwell on that now. If they didn't get off the ship soon, she'd find herself back in London with no way to return.

"Do you want anything else in here?" asked Alice, holding out the sack toward Rommy, who took it and placed the food inside it.

"So's how do you propose we get out of here without anyone seeing us? It's broad daylight, and all them men is probably scurrying all over out there if they's ready to ship out and all."

"Maybe if everyone is busy, that will help," said Rommy. "We just have to look like we are supposed to be out there. If we look like we are sneaking, someone will notice, for sure. Just follow my lead."

She walked over to the door, but the knob wouldn't turn in her hand. She jiggled it and then pulled on it. "No!" she said. "I can't believe it! Mr. Smee locked us in!" She clenched her hands and let out a groan. Unlike her father's cabin, there was no handy porthole window out of which to escape.

With all the ideas going through her head for how to get off the ship without being seen, Rommy hadn't even considered what she would do if her cabin was locked. And she couldn't believe she hadn't! She dropped on the bed and put her face in her hands. Her nose prickled with unshed tears.

"I am so stupid!"

A small hand patted her shoulder. "You ain't stupid," said Alice, "but you sure are a watering pot today. You got one of those hair things around here?"

Rommy gave a watery laugh and wiped at her eyes. She moved over to the trunk. Her best friend Francie had shoved so many pins into her hair when she left Chattingham's trying to make her look like a boy, that even despite all Rommy had gone through to find her father, there were still a few left. She only hoped Smee had put them with her other things and they weren't sitting somewhere in her father's cabin.

Her fingers brushed a small parchment packet, and she pulled it out. Inside were four hair pins. Rommy let out the breath she had been holding and handed the packet to Alice. Alice fished out one of the pins and then knelt in front of the door.

"I don't think that will work," said Rommy, standing behind her. "I tried to pick the lock the last time Papa locked me in his cabin."

"You're standing in my light," said Alice, her face screwed up in concentration.

Rommy backed up, sat back down on the bed, and watched as Alice moved the hair pin first one way and then another. A soft click sounded and Alice turned around and grinned.

"This ain't my first door, you know" she said. She pushed the pin back into the little packet and tossed it toward Rommy. "You'd better put them in the sack, too. No telling when they might come in handy again."

Alice moved to open the door, but Rommy stopped her. "Wait! This cabin opens toward the side of the ship. We need to be careful when we slip out so it looks normal." She rolled the sack up as tightly as she could and put it under her arm. "We're going to stroll over to the railing like we're interested in what's going on. Then when nobody's looking, we'll slip over the rail."

Rommy cracked the door open and peered around the edge. She could see down the side of the ship toward the main deck. It was alive with men moving back and forth and the noise of the crew making ready to leave. Her eyes darted around to find her father. She certainly didn't want to run into him.

Finally, she spotted him at the bow of the boat. His back was toward her, and he was chewing out Mr. Smee. She gestured to Alice to follow her, and the two slipped silently out of the cabin door. Rommy casually stood outside and ambled toward the railing. Alice followed her example. The men on deck seemed oblivious to the two girls' presence. Rommy leaned against the rail, looking up toward the men bustling around.

She rose to hover just above the deck when Tommy, the cabin boy, rounded the corner. She thumped back to the planking.

For a moment, he looked confused. Rommy knew her panic was written all over her face, and she tried to smooth it out. She gave a tentative smile and turned so that the sack was behind her. She felt Alice tug it out of her hands.

"Wotcha doing out here?" asked Tommy. "The Captain, he said I was to bring you this." The boy held out a round pot. Rommy felt her face color.

"Oh, well, thank you," she said, but she didn't reach out to take it.

Tommy tilted his head as he awkwardly held the pot between them. "Uh, do you want me to put it in Smee's, I mean your cabin?"

"Why, yes," said Rommy and then felt Alice kick her. "I mean, no."

She reached for the pot just as Tommy tucked it under his arm. The boy, clearly confused, pulled it out again as Rommy dropped her hands.

"Oh for the love of Pete," burst out Alice, stepping from behind Rommy. "Here, give it to me," she said, plucking the pot from Tommy's grasp. "We was just coming out to find this, so you saved us the trouble."

The boy's face cleared, relief evident. "Okay," he said. "That's that. I'll let the Captain know I delivered it to you."

"You do that," said Alice. "Let him know we were right glad to get it, too."

As Tommy walked away, Rommy leaned over to Alice. "What are you doing?" she whispered.

"I'm saving us from being caught," said Alice with a little huff. "You looked like a fish flopping on the dock, opening and closing your mouth like that."

"No, I mean, why did you tell him to give my father a message?"

"Oh, that." Alice smiled. "If he has to remember a message, he'll probably forget to say where we was."

Rommy squeezed Alice's shoulder. "Good thinking!"

Rommy glanced back at the deck, which was still buzzing with activity, and then bent and picked up the sack Alice had put up against the wall. "We'd better get going before we run into anyone else." A smile lifted one side of her mouth. "Even you will have a hard time explaining why we are walking around with a chamber pot!"

The two girls made the short trip to the deck railing and slid over, Alice rather awkwardly, as her small arms struggled to hold onto the chamber pot.

Rommy flew toward the back of the ship, near the water line. Alice followed her and then nodded at the object in her arms. "What do you want me to do with this thing?" The little girl made to drop it into the water, but Rommy stopped her.

"No, hang on to it, at least until the ship leaves," she said. "If anyone sees it floating in the water, it will make him suspicious."

"But it's heavy," said Alice.

"We'll switch," said Rommy, taking the pot from Alice and handing her the sack. It didn't take long before the pot seemed to have become twice as heavy. She readjusted it in her arms and leaned against the side of the ship.

"Now what?" asked Alice, hovering next to Rommy.

"Now, we wait," said Rommy.

Chapter 20:
Little Owl's Help

Rommy was starting to wonder how long she would have to hold the chamber pot when Alice's eyes went wide.

"Look," she said, pointing at the ship behind Rommy's left shoulder. Rommy turned and felt her mouth drop open.

Golden lines were running over all the seams of every piece of wood. Within a minute, the entire ship was glowing.

"Blimey," said Alice. "I ain't seen nothing like that before."

Rommy shook her head. "I haven't, either. I suppose it must be the pixie dust." She and Alice exchanged a look. "I wonder how it works."

Before she could wonder further, the ship gave a creak and a groan and moved forward. As it strained ahead, it slowly rose until the hull skimmed the top of the waves. Water dripped from the bottom, and it picked up speed, lifting higher as it went.

"Quick," said Rommy and grabbing Alice's arm, she pulled them both until they were flying beneath the big ship, keeping pace with it. Alice made a face as water plopped onto her head and ran down the side of her neck.

"How long do we hafta stay under here?" she asked, wrinkling her nose. "And what about that pot?" She pointed to the round object still in Rommy's arms.

"Nobody will notice it now," said Rommy and dropped it into the waves, glad to be rid of the cumbersome thing.

She tugged at Alice's hand, and the two girls put on a burst of speed to stay underneath the boat as it flew higher and faster. When they reached the rocky shoreline, Rommy pointed downwards, and they dropped onto the ground and ducked behind a boulder. They watched as the ship flew away, climbing higher in the sky the farther it traveled. Rommy hoped her father would be so taken up with steering the ship that he wouldn't think to check on her until much, much later.

Alice moved forward, but Rommy put her hand on her shoulder. "Wait," she said. "Once they're out of sight, we can just fly. It won't take nearly as long as trying to walk over all these rocks."

Alice settled down on the ground and leaned her head back against the boulder that shielded them from view. She looked up at Rommy, who was still watching the ship as it became a mere speck in the sky.

"I'll say this for you," she said. "You sure ain't boring. I ain't had this much adventure in, well, never."

Rommy made a face. "I'd take a bit of boring right about now. I have an idea things will get even more exciting from here on out." She let out a sigh as she watched her father's ship fade from view. "Come on! I don't think anyone will see us now."

Alice pushed up to her feet, and the girls leaped into the air and flew the now-familiar route toward Chief Hawk Eye's encampment. As they got near, Rommy signaled and the two girls touched down in the long grasses that grew on this area of the island. Rommy could see the conical homes all clustered in a circle around a main fire pit, encircled by big flat rocks. The late morning sun lit the clearing and highlighted the people moving around the area. There were too many to risk trying to find Little Owl.

"What are we waiting for?" asked Alice.

"There are too many people around right now," said Rommy.

"How long do you think we'll hafta wait?" asked Alice.

"I'm not sure, but you should probably get comfortable." Both girls sighed as they sat down in the tall grasses.

Time ticked by slowly, and the sun beat down on their heads. Finally, Rommy heard a commotion. She peered back toward the small village and saw Chief Hawk Eye, Little Bear and two other men striding out of the camp. The two men had spears over their shoulders and the Chief carried a long bow. She wasn't sure where Little Owl or Tiger Lily were, but the area around the fire pit was empty.

"Can we go now?" asked Alice.

Rommy hesitated, looking at the homes around the central fire pit. "I'm not sure which one is Little Owl's," she admitted.

Alice waved a hand. "Oh, that's easy," she said. "Follow me."

The two girls circled around to the back of the encampment and crept toward the home that Alice pointed out. How the girl could tell it apart from the others, Rommy had no idea; she only hoped Alice was right.

As they crouched in the grass, Rommy wondered how they would get to Little Owl. It was still early enough that she didn't think they should go around to the front. Even if they called to the older woman, what if someone else was in there with her? What if someone heard them?

"What are you scowling at?" asked Alice, lifting an eyebrow.

"I'm trying to figure out how we're going to let Little Owl know we're here without anyone else finding out," said Rommy blowing out a breath. "Just once, it'd be wonderful if something was simple on this cursed island."

Alice shook her head. "Why didn't you say so?" She cupped both hands over her mouth and made a hooting sound. She did three quick hoots, paused, and then let one long hoot.

Rommy stared at her.

Alice smiled, her dimple showing. "Little Owl and I got some signals together. You know, just in case."

"Oh, Alice, I could hug you right now!" said Rommy, a grin spreading over her face.

Sure enough, a few minutes later, they saw Little Owl coming around the side of her home, her eyes searching the long grasses. Alice popped up and waved, grinning.

The woman hurried to the back of her tent and loosened one of the long polished wooden stakes that held it down. "Hurry," she said, her voice soft, as she waved Alice and Rommy under the opening.

The girls squirmed through and then stood. It wasn't long until the tent flap opened and Little Owl entered. She looked from one to the other.

"I am guessing you did not come to visit?"

Rommy and Alice looked at each other, and Rommy stepped forward. "We were hoping you could help us, Little

Owl. We need to speak with Unilisi and find out how to close that passage to Neverland."

Little Owl sank into the rocking chair by the fire and shook her head. "I thought that was why you came, but you cannot go into the jungle alone, the two of you. It is folly."

Rommy came to kneel by the older woman. "My father has left Neverland, and he thinks I'm on his ship. Once he realizes I'm gone, he'll come back. I don't know how long that will take, but I have to find Unilisi and get her to tell me how to close off Neverland before he returns." Rommy leaned forward.

Little Owl put a gnarled hand on Rommy's cheek. "So much fire for one so young," she said and shook her head. "But even as fierce as you are, you will never survive the journey. This island," she said, waving a hand, "it has a terrible beauty, one that kills. The few who have gone into the jungle unprepared don't return."

Rommy felt a shiver slide up her spine. She swallowed. "I have to try," she said. "Papa was going to take Alice and me back to London and hide us away again. He's spent a decade trying to get Pan, and I don't want to spend another decade waiting for him, worrying about him." Her voice broke. "I can't." She looked down as she felt tears well up in her eyes.

"Oh, Child," said Little Owl, the sympathy in her voice undoing Rommy, who blinked rapidly to keep the tears from falling.

Alice patted Rommy's shoulder and then looked at Little Owl. "So's, if we can't go by ourselves, who *can* help us? I don't want to turn up my toes," Alice said, jerking a thumb in Rommy's direction, "but her old man ain't leaving this place if Pan's still going about his merry business."

Rommy sniffed and wiped at her eyes. "I'm sorry," she said. "It all seems so hopeless. Papa won't let me help him, and Pan won't stop stealing children. If we can stop him, if we can close off Neverland, we'll stop Pan, and I'll get my father back. Don't you see? I have to do this!"

Little Owl stared into Rommy's eyes for a long moment before giving a brisk nod of her head. "Yes, I can see that you do," she said. Placing her hands on her knees, she pushed up from the rocker. "But you'll need some help. Little Bear would be a good companion on this journey, but when your father returns, he mustn't suspect any of us helped you, or he will become very angry. And Captain Hook's temper is its own beast." The old woman placed a finger to her lips and tapped several times. Suddenly, her face brightened. "But I think I know who can help you."

Without another word, the older woman hurried out of tent, leaving Rommy and Alice looking at each other. A small glimmer of hope burned between them.

Chapter 21:
Preparing for a Journey

The minutes crawled by as Rommy and Alice waited for Little Owl to return. Alice sat down on the rocking chair, but Rommy was too nervous to sit. Instead, she walked around the perimeter of the tidy dwelling, taking in the simple furniture and several paintings done on what looked like tree bark.

She leaned over one, studying the detail of an enormous tree surrounded by thousands of lights, each a different tint. When she looked closer, she could see each light was a tiny being. It took a moment for her to realize that she was looking at fairies. She wondered if the fairies lived in the tree and if the tree was real. Before she could investigate further, the flap flew open and Little Owl hurried in, followed by several balls of light.

One zoomed to hover right in front of Rommy's face, and she recognized Nissa. She smiled tentatively. The fairy had not always seemed to like her very much. "Hello, Nissa," she said. She gave small wave and then felt foolish.

Nissa clicked and trilled at her and then flew over to Alice, settling on the younger girl's shoulder. Alice giggled.

"The fairies will lead you and protect you," said Little Owl. "You know Nissa." She turned and gestured to three other balls of light. Each was a different hue. Pointing to one with an amber tone, she said, "This is Balo. He has a special bond with the animals of the jungle." Two glowing balls moved forward together, one tinted green and the other silver. "These are Kalen and Talen," she said. "They are both warrior fairies. They are small, but they will protect you. Together, these four should be able to get you where you need to go and return you safely."

Rommy looked at each small creature and felt a pang of unease. "But, how will we communicate with them?" She put up a hand when Nissa made an ominous buzzing sound. "Not that I'm ungrateful for their help, nor do I doubt their abilities. But how will they be able to keep us safe or guide us if we can't understand each other?"

Little Owl smiled. "They can understand you well enough, but you bring up a good point." She turned and went over to her sleeping cot. Gingerly getting down on her knees, she reached way underneath the bed and pulled out a carved stone box. Holding it close to her heart, she pushed herself up to stand. She placed the object on the quilt and opened the lid. Inside, something cast a warm glow, but Rommy couldn't see what it was until Little Owl turned. In her hand was a glowing dark green stone attached to a leather cord. She stepped over and placed it over Rommy's head. When the stone touched Rommy skin, it felt warm and almost like it was pulsing. Tentatively, she touched it and then looked up, startled, when Nissa buzzed into her face.

She was even more surprised when, instead of clicking and trilling, she heard a clear, melodious voice. "We will take you to Unilisi, but we won't promise that she'll talk to you," the fairy said.

Rommy stared at Nissa and then down at the stone. "Does this...how...what...?

"I hope you are more intelligent than this on our journey," said a deeper voice that still managed to sound musical. One of the other fairies, the one Little Owl had called Balo, was now also hovering in front of her face. This close, Rommy could see his auburn hair and golden eyes. Unlike Nissa, he seemed thicker and more muscular. He had a scowl on his tiny face.

Little Owl chuckled. "Now, Balo, the girls are not from here. You cannot expect them to know what a hearing stone is if they have never seen one before."

The fairy made a sound that was suspiciously close to a har-rumph. "What she knows or doesn't is irrelevant. We must be ready to leave at first light."

Little Owl's face became serious. "You are right, Balo," she said. Turning to Rommy and Alice, she said, "I will put togeth-er some things for you, but you must be ready to leave before dawn. It is imperative that nobody knows you've been here."

"Why can't we leave now?" asked Rommy.

A tinkle of laughter sounded in her ears. "Do you want to die, human?" asked the one Little Owl had called Talen. "The jungle is always dangerous, but by the time we are ready to leave, the sun will be setting. Once it is dark, it will be more challenging to keep you safe. It's better if we have time to plan a protected place to rest."

"She is right, but we have much to do," said Little Owl. "I also must prepare you to meet Unilisi. She is not to be trifled with, and she will be unwilling to listen if you don't approach her in the correct way."

Alice rolled her eyes. "This tree lady sounds like a right git. Ain't there nobody else we can ask?"

Little Owl smiled and laid a hand on the young girl's head. "No, little one, there is no one else, but we will prepare and hope. Sometimes, that is enough. Now, you must listen, and then you may rest until it is safe to leave."

The older woman settled herself into the rocker. Alice and Rommy sat at her feet, and the fairies drew closer, too, alighting around the elderly woman.

"Now, listen," said Little Owl.

Chapter 22:
Best-Laid Plans and All That

Rommy and Alice nestled in a pile of blankets clustered around the central fire in Little Owl's home. Rommy could hear Alice's gentle snores, signaling the younger girl had already dropped off to sleep.

Rommy was not having the same luck. She stared up at the pointed ceiling, Little Owl's instructions about Unilisi turning over and over in her head. She wished she could relax and go to sleep, but her stomach was tied into a tight knot. What if she failed? What if she dragged Alice through the dangerous jungle and it was all for nothing? Worse, what if something happened to Alice along the way?

At Chattingham's Rommy had listened to a lecture given by an intrepid woman explorer. She, along with her classmates, had sat enthralled as the woman regaled them with her spine-tingling adventures deep in the Congo of Africa. Rommy remembered being glad that she, at least, was sitting in a chair in London and not traipsing through a jungle a continent away.

In the dark, her mouth quirked at the irony. If only she'd known. The thing was, as dangerous as those jungles back in her world were, the jungles of Neverland were worse. Not only were there the typical wild animals and snakes, but there were also plants that could kill and deadly magical creatures.

That didn't even take into account Unilisi. She sounded not only wholly uninterested in the problems of Neverland's inhabitants but also somewhat hostile. Rommy only prayed that the tree woman—or whatever she was—would be in a good mood when they finally found her. If she wasn't, Rommy wasn't sure what to do.

Rommy's eyes flew open. She must have drifted off after all. She looked around the dark living area and felt Alice stir beside her. What had woken her?

Then she heard it again. An urgent voice. "Little Owl? Rommy?"

The entrance flap cracked open, and moonlight filtered onto the floor. Rommy blinked. It must still be night. She wondered how long she had slept. A head poked in, and before she could identify who it was, a shadow shot across the swath of moonlight.

Rommy sat up and stared. Little Owl was sitting on the back of whoever had opened the tent flap and had the person immobilized. By this time, Alice was sitting up and rubbing her eyes.

"What's going on?" she said, her voice still sleepy.

Rommy got to her feet just as the person croaked out, "It's me, Finn. Let me up!"

Little Owl eased back. "Forgive me," she said, helping Finn to his feet.

Finn dusted himself off and shook his head. "Wow, I didn't know you could do that," he said. He stretched his neck, and it audibly cracked.

Little Owl chuckled and shook a finger at him. "You thought I was too old, but there is still life in these old bones." She quickly became serious. "Now, what has you coming here at this hour of the night?"

"I came to warn you," said Finn.

"Warn us?" A look of alarm spread over Little Owl's face.

"Yeah, um..." Finn looked away from the older woman and pulled in a deep breath. "I'm sorry to say it, but Tiger Lily overheard your plans and told Pan. He's planning on stopping the girls before they can even get to the jungle."

Rommy couldn't help her sharp inhalation. "No," she said, "we can't let him do that!"

Finn shrugged. "If you don't want him to, you're going to have to leave right now. He was still at the caves when I left, but I'm sure he's left by now"

Alice was already pulling out the two packs Little Owl had helped them prepare earlier. She shoved her feet into the soft shoes that Little Owl had made for her and came to stand by Rommy, who hadn't moved yet.

"We can go now," said Alice.

"But, what about what the fairies said about the jungle at night?" asked Rommy, a sense of panic washing over her. What if they forgot something? What if they got turned around in the dark? What if...she snapped back to the moment when Alice shook her arm.

"Rommy? Hello, Rommy? Get your stuff. Little Owl has water and food for us."

Rommy blinked at Alice and then at Little Owl, who was holding out two water flasks and a small bundle wrapped in cloth. "You can eat this once you are in the jungle" said Little Owl. "There's no time to lose."

Looking at Rommy's white face, Little Owl touched her arm. "Everything will be fine," the older woman said, her voice soothing. "But you need to hurry now. Once you get into the jungle, Pan won't have an easy time finding you, even if he follows you in, which is doubtful. He has enemies in the jungle, so he will probably try to stop you before you get there."

Rommy's panicked paralysis lifted. She took the food and water from Little Owl and spun to grab her boots. She pulled them on and quickly re-braided her hair, which had come halfway undone. Turning, she squared her shoulders.

"I'm ready," she said. "Where are the fairies?"

"We've been waiting for you," said Balo. "Humans! Always so slow." He spun in the air and headed toward the entrance. When he realized nobody was following him, he let out a harrumph and hovered by the doorway, his tiny arms crossed. He looked so grumpy, Rommy had to stifle a somewhat hysterical giggle.

Finn looked at Little Owl. "What will you tell them?" he asked. "I know you wanted to get the girls out of here without anyone knowing they had been here, but I doubt Tiger Lily will keep this to herself."

Little Owl smiled. "Don't you worry about that, young man. I can handle everyone here. But you must all go. Now." She herded them all toward the door, where the four fairies were waiting.

Rommy stopped and spun toward Finn. "But, Finn, what about you? Won't Pan know you warned us if we're gone before he gets here? Won't he notice you're missing?"

Finn grimaced. "It don't matter, now," he said.

"What do you mean?" she asked.

"I can't go back now," said Finn. "I had to make a choice, and Pan has to be stopped. You were right about that. This is the only way to do it." He shrugged. "I guess you have someone else in your little party now."

Rommy stared at Finn for a long moment. "That was a really brave thing to do," she said. She laid her hand on his arm when Finn looked away. "No, I mean it. I know you are really worried about the other Lost Boys, but I think it's the best way to protect them—in the long run."

A smile tipped Finn's lips and even in the dark she could see his face darkening. Suddenly, Rommy felt a shove from behind her.

"Will the two of you get moving already?" said Alice. "You've got the whole long walk through the jungle to stare at each other."

Rommy felt her face grow warm when she saw the twinkle in Little Owl's eyes. The older woman steered them out and around the back of her home. The sky was still dark, but the moon wasn't quite as high as it had been, and the stars were winking out.

"You must hurry," the older woman said. She placed a hand on Rommy's head. "May the spirit of good fortune go with you." She moved her hand to her heart. "I feel that your journey will bring the answers you seek."

The older woman fumbled at her waist and then pushed something at Rommy. When her hand closed around it, Rommy realized it was Little Owl's dagger still in its sheath.

Rommy blinked back unexpected tears and quickly fastened the sheath to her waistband before she flinging her arms around the older woman. "Thank you," she said into her ear. "I won't forget this."

With a last look at the older woman, Rommy followed Finn and the fairies as they pushed into the air, heading toward the cliffs where the jungle waited.

Chapter 23:
Into the Jungle

The group landed on the edge of the cliffs. Rommy had spent the entire time flying here tense, waiting for Pan to show up, but Finn had warned them in time. Still, they weren't safe yet.

She looked to where the jungle abruptly started only a few feet away. Even here, at the beginning of the path, it was overgrown.

"We can't fly in most of the jungle," said Finn. "The trees and plants all grow too close together, but there is a bit of a path through most of it. The big thing is, we can't get off the path, or we'll never find our way out again."

Rommy looked up at the towering trees crowding out the sky. Long tangles of vines dripped off the branches, straggling onto the ground and creeping toward the cliff's edge.

"Why can't we just fly over the top and then land close to Unilisi's grove?" she asked. It seemed much less intimidating than trying to walk through the crowded vegetation. It also seemed safer.

"'Fly over the top,' she says. 'Land in the middle of the jungle,' she says." Balo's laugh wasn't pleasant. "I know you are a human, but I didn't know you were quite so stupid."

"Hey," said Rommy.

Balo came to hover in front of Rommy's face, his glow getting brighter. "Don't you know anything, you big, dumb girl?" The fairy held up one finger. "First, Pan will see you, and you'll be a nice, bright target."

Rommy felt her face flush. She hadn't thought of that, only of trying to avoid the dark depths of the wildness before her.

Balo held up another finger. "Second, you can't just go through the canopy all willy-nilly. Well, we can." He pointed to his fellow fairies and then gestured at Rommy, Alice, and Finn. "But *you* can't. You're too big. You'd get caught in the branches of one of the guardian trees. Even if you made it through there, which is highly doubtful, the birds or the monkeys would get you."

"What's he saying?" asked Alice, wrinkling her nose.

Rommy explained what Balo had said, and Alice wrinkled her nose. "Why do we gots to be afraid of birds and monkeys?"

"Because, you dimwitted child, they guard the jungle, and they don't welcome uninvited guests, especially ones that drop in from the sky."

"Balo," said Nissa, coming to hover by him. "We are wasting time. I think you've made your point." She turned to Rommy. "We must go through the jungle. There are no shortcuts." She tilted her head. "But it was a valid question, despite Balo's blustering."

The two warrior fairies were now waiting at the start of the path. "Come, we must hurry," said the male one. Rommy couldn't remember if he was Kalen or Talen.

His sister pointed with her tiny spear. "Kalen is right," she said, scanning the sky behind them. Rommy mentally made a note that the sister was Talen and the brother was Kalen. "Our luck has held so far, but we must go before Pan finds us."

Kalen and Balo led the way. The path was so narrow and overgrown Rommy and Alice had to walk single-file behind him. Nissa hovered by Finn, who was behind the girls, and Talen brought up the rear.

Stepping into the jungle was like entering a tunnel. They had only gone a few feet when the light from the moon disappeared completely. The air felt close and plants brushed against Rommy's hair, face, and body. She hoped none of them was carnivorous or poisonous. She was thankful for her boots because it was impossible to see where she was stepping. Alice clutched the back of her shirt, and Rommy felt a stab of guilt. Maybe the little girl would have been better off with Little Owl.

The group moved silently, but the surrounding jungle was alive with the night creatures that lived there. A cacophony of insect noises, along with hoots and whistles filled the night air. The undergrowth swayed and rustled as larger creatures moved through the jungle.

"This place is kinda spooky," said Alice, her voice barely a whisper.

"We'll be okay if we all stay together and on the path," said Finn, his voice floating from somewhere behind them.

Rommy wasn't sure how long they had been following the glowing amber and green balls of light when she realized it was getting lighter. The trees and plants were now dim outlines rather than just shadows. Gradually, the world around her became clearer.

The trees thinned out a bit, and Balo and Kalen came to a stop.

"What are we stopping for?" Rommy asked, although she was grateful. Her mouth was dry and her legs were tired.

"We will take a moment to rest and refresh ourselves," said Kalen with a stern glance at Balo, who had let out a loud huff. Kalen flew over to a tree that was lying next to the path, inspecting it from one end to the other and even flying through the hollowed trunk. He came out and hovered in front of Rommy. "It is safe," he said. "You may sit and eat. The small one needs this stop."

Rommy, Alice, and Finn didn't need any more encouragement. The three of them plopped down on the log, and Rommy opened the pack to pull out the cloth-wrapped bundle and the water flasks. She looked at Finn. "We'll have to share the water. Little Owl only gave us the two."

Finn shrugged. "I'm fine."

Rommy unwrapped the cloth and found six small biscuit-sized pieces of food. She gave two each to Finn and Alice. All three of them started to eat immediately. After several bites, Rommy stopped and looked at the fairies.

"I'm so sorry," she said, embarrassed. "Can we share with you?"

Nissa made a face. "No, but we thank you." The twin fairies nodded at Rommy. Nissa poked Balo.

He waved a hand. "Like we would want human food." He said human food in the same tone one might say garbage. Rommy bit back a smile. For some reason, she found Balo's extreme grumpiness amusing.

Rommy finished the last of her biscuits, took a swallow of water, and put the flask into her shirt pocket. She leaned down to pick up the sack by her foot and felt a whoosh above her head. There was a loud thunk as something solid hit the tree behind her.

Before she could turn to see what it was, Finn had tackled both her and Alice and rolled them behind the log. She spit out a mouthful of moss.

"What..."

"Sssh," he said, poking his head above the log. Another whistling sound and another thunk. "Blast!" he said.

Rommy was still confused. "What's going on?" she said.

Finn met her eyes, his mouth pressed into a thin line. "Someone is shooting at us."

"Is it Pan?" asked Alice, her face white.

Finn opened his mouth to answer, but Nissa buzzed down to the hover in front of them. "You must run," she said. "Kalen, Talen, and I will hold off the girl. Follow Balo. He will lead you, for you must leave the path. Follow him now, quickly, when you hear the signal."

The three of them pulled their feet underneath them and prepared to make a run for it. Suddenly, a loud undulating war cry sounded. Without waiting to see who had made it, Finn tucked Alice under his arm and pulled Rommy after him. They crashed through the undergrowth, struggling to keep Balo's golden brown light in view.

Rommy was running blind, and the only thing that kept her from falling several times was Finn's hand grasping hers. She didn't know how he was running so fast and holding onto Alice. Although she tried to protect her face, leaves and branches slapped at her and tore at her hair.

She leaped over a log, and then Finn disappeared and his hand tore out of her grasp. Before she could figure out what had happened, she stepped into nothing. Her arms cart-wheeled, trying to grab onto anything, but there was just empty space.

Chapter 24:
Wolf Pack

Branches and vines caught at Rommy's hair as she tumbled through the air, too shocked even to try to fly. She landed with a thud, and for a moment, she couldn't breathe. She sucked frantically at the air, but nothing went into her lungs.

A face appeared, scrunched into worry. "Are you okay? Why are you gawping like a fish?" Alice asked.

"She's just got the wind knocked out of her, is all," said Finn, who put his arm behind Rommy's back and helped her to sit up. She shook her head and looked around her. They were in some kind of ravine that was choked with vines and plants growing at all angles. "Well, I wasn't expecting that," she said when she could breathe again.

Finn put out his hand, and she allowed him to pull her up to her feet. "Where are Nissa and the others?" she asked, realizing that the lights she had become used to were absent.

Finn pointed upward. Rommy followed his movement and saw four glowing lights hovering on the far side of the ravine's edge. The amber light buzzed down toward them.

"What are you doing down here?" Balo demanded.

"We certainly didn't plan to end up down here," Rommy said.

"Well, don't dawdle. This is not a place you want to..."

A low growl interrupted him. Balo threw up his tiny arms. "Here we go," he muttered.

Alice tapped Rommy's arm. "Rommy? I think we gots problems," she said.

Rommy turned her head, and her stomach dropped. Six massive wolves had arranged themselves around them, three on each end of the ravine, blocking any escape. She looked up, and all she could see were tangles of vegetation. Maybe if they pushed up hard enough, they could fly through it without getting caught.

Balo flew toward the largest wolf, holding out his arms in a placating gesture. "Now, Bardolf," he said. "The younglings didn't mean to intrude on your territory. It was quite an accident on their part, and they are happy to leave right away."

Rommy looked from one wolf to the next. They all mostly looked alike, their fur a mixture of gray and black. However, the smallest one had fur that was a pale silvery gray, and one wolf was so black he seemed part of the shadows.

Four of the wolves had their heads lowered, teeth bared, fur bristling, but the small, silver one was just staring at them. The big black one wasn't snarling, but his eyes, a startling blue, pierced into them as if waiting for them to make a wrong move.

Finn, Alice, and Rommy moved closer together, their backs touching each other. As if on cue, all the wolves took another step closer, tightening the circle.

Balo moved toward the wolf he had called Bardolf. "You know they mean no harm, here," said Balo.

"What are these human younglings doing in the jungle, anyway?" growled Bardolf. "If you can answer that to my satisfaction, I may let them leave."

Rommy had been listening to the exchange, and she took a tentative step forward. One wolf, a whip thin animal with glowing yellow eyes, snapped her jaws and growled deep in its throat. Rommy became still, not even turning her head toward Bardolf.

"We apologize for intruding," she said, her lips barely moving, her eyes trained on the snarling wolf. "Our only wish is to talk to Unilisi, and we'd be very grateful if you would allow us to leave."

Bardolf's eyes widened, and his muzzle wrinkled in confusion. "You can understand me, youngling?" he asked.

Rommy nodded her head and tugged the glowing stone from beneath her shirt. "I was given a hearing stone," she said. She wasn't sure what the relationship between Chief Hawk Eye's people and the wolves was, so she didn't mention Little Owl's name.

"Hmm, I have not seen one of those in a long while, but then few humans venture this deeply into the jungle," he said. He looked around at the others and gave a sharp yip. The other wolves visibly relaxed. The big black one sat down on his haunches.

Bardolf padded forward until he stood in front of Rommy. He was so large he could look her straight in the eye. She swallowed and became very still.

Behind the wolf's massive head, Balo motioning at her to not move.

"Why are you going to see the Tree Mother? Don't you know this is a very dangerous place for a youngling?" Bardolf leaned forward and sniffed at Rommy.

Rommy held her breath until the wolf pulled his snout away from her. She wasn't sure what she should or shouldn't say, but the wolf waited for her to speak. Taking a deep breath, she decided to just tell the truth.

"We want to see if Unilisi knows of a way to close the passage from our world to Neverland," she said. "Peter Pan is bringing children here against their will, and we want to stop him."

"Fewer humans can only be a good thing," said a more feminine voice. It was the thin wolf. "But how do we know she speaks the truth?"

Bardolf frowned at the other wolf. "Tala, not every human is an enemy, but you are right. Fewer humans would be better for the island, and the human called Peter has never been a friend to us." He turned back to Rommy. "How did your elders allow you, a group of younglings, to make this journey? Even with the fairy folk, your chances of getting to the Tree Mother and back out alive are not promising."

Rommy lifted her chin. "We have to try," she said. "We can't let Pan keep kidnapping children. It's just wrong."

The black wolf stood and came forward. He lowered his head to Bardolf. Bardolf placed his head on top of the black wolf's and rubbed it with his chin. Then he stepped back half a pace.

The black wolf turned to inspect Rommy. His blue eyes unnerved her, and he was almost as tall as Bardolf, but he was bulkier. She resisted the urge to back up. He swung his head back to the leader of the pack.

"Bardolf, perhaps we should aid these younglings in their journey," he said. "As you say, the jungle is dangerous. The fairies are powerful, but there are many dangerous creatures here."

Bardolf tilted his head and studied the black wolf. "You may be right, Lobo." He turned his head to another gray wolf, this one slim and graceful. "Artemis, what do you think, my dear? Shall we escort these younglings on their quest?"

The she-wolf paced forward and nuzzled her mate. "You are generous, Bardolf, to think of helping the humans, but we shouldn't put the entire pack at risk." Her eyes swung to Lobo. "Perhaps we can send one wolf along with them, to help guard them and keep them safe."

Bardolf nosed the she-wolf. "As always, you are wise, my love," he said. He looked around at the other wolves, who had all drawn closer, listening in on the conversation.

The one called Tala curled her lip, and Rommy hoped Bardolf wouldn't volunteer that wolf to go with them. She'd have to sleep with one eye open. The silvery wolf had lost interest and was stalking something in a clump of bushes. Another wolf was on his belly. He seemed to be trying to make himself smaller. A low whine came from between his lips.

Bardolf looked at Artemis. "We can't send Luna," he said. "She is still too much a cub."

"I believe the only choice is Lobo," said Artemis. "Tala doesn't care for humans, and Phalon," she curled her lip, "I don't think he is up for the task." The wolf on his belly whined louder.

Lobo stepped closer to the alpha pair and bowed his head. "It would honor me to take the younglings to the Tree Mother," he said. His tail swished back and forth.

Bardolf stepped away from Artemis and turned his attention once more to Rommy. "Lobo will go with you, and he will help to keep you safe."

Rommy wasn't sure she wanted a wolf as a traveling companion, but there wasn't anything she could do about it at this point. She bowed her head respectfully. "I thank you for your generosity and your kindness," she said.

Bardolf nudged her shoulder with his nose. "Go now with Lobo," he said. "He will show you how to get out of the ravine."

Finn had been watching the exchange, his eyes moving from Bardolf to Rommy. Alice, who was between Finn and Rommy, had remained silent, although her small body was stiff with tension.

Rommy turned and explained what had just happened. Finn lifted an eyebrow. "The wolf pack wants to help us?" he asked incredulously.

"Ain't it a bad idea to bring along something that can eat you?" said Alice.

Rommy knew the hearing stone made her words plain to Bardolf, but she didn't think it would interpret what Alice and Finn were saying. Still, she didn't want to offend Bardolf or seem ungrateful for his offer of help. "Bardolf is kindly sending Lobo with us. We should be very grateful for his help."

Balo, who had also been watching the proceedings with interest, zipped up and smacked Finn on the back of his head. "Are you stupid, boy? Take the wolves up on their offer and don't sound ungrateful. Lobo will be a great help on this journey, and he is not averse to humans the way Tala is. Now, let's go. We've wasted enough time as it is."

The big black wolf padded up to stand next to Rommy. "I will do my best to lead you and protect you," he said. "You have my promise."

Rommy decided she would trust him unless he gave her a reason not to. After all, what choice did she have? "Thank you, Lobo," she said. Then she gestured with her hand. "We'll follow you."

With a soft woof, the big black wolf moved forward, and Rommy, Finn, and Alice followed him through the snaking ravine. Rommy just hoped this wasn't a mistake.

Chapter 25:
Traveling Jungle-Style

Lobo led the small group unerringly though the dense brush and rocky ground out of the ravine. Rommy had to admit they would have had a hard time finding their way without him. When they reached the top, Lobo paused and looked at Rommy. She turned to the others, who had all stopped and gathered into a circle. They were all now staring at her. Expectant. A fizz of nerves started in her stomach.

"I'm wondering if we should go back to the main path or not," she said. "Do you know who was shooting at us?" she asked, suspecting the answer.

Nissa moved forward. "It was Tiger Lily," she said. "I believe it is wiser to stay off the path. She will expect you to follow it. You will be much easier targets there."

Balo scoffed. "She probably thinks you were wolf snacks and left."

Finn kicked at a stone and sent it tumbling down the side of the ravine. "I don't know, Balo. Pan probably sent her to do his dirty work, and he'll want proof we're no longer a problem."

Balo snorted. "We can't go traipsing through the jungle with you two and the child. Even with the warrior fairies that would be a challenge."

Nissa let out an exasperated sigh. "Balo, must you always argue about everything? Tiger Lily will be looking for us on the main path."

Lobo, who had sat on his haunches once they had reached the top, now stood up. "I can lead you through the jungle," he said. "We will need to be very careful, but you are less likely to face attack. It will be safer."

"Safer for who?" said Balo, flying to hover in front of the wolf's face.

Finn glanced from Rommy to Lobo, a frown creasing his face. "It seems to me that if Tiger Lily is in here, trying to get rid of us, we'd be fools to make it easy for her."

"But how're we supposed to know where to go?" asked Alice. She was standing as close to Rommy as she could and scanning the surrounding forest, flinching with every sound. "Seems to me, our goose is cooked, either way. I think being eaten would be worse than being shot."

Lobo, hearing the fear in the little girl's voice leaned his head down and nuzzled her. Alice froze. The wolf licked her cheek, and a smile started on the little girl's face, her dimple peeking out. She tentatively put her hand in his fur and patted. He wagged his tail.

"I think we should let Lobo lead us," said Rommy. "Even though there are dangers off the path, I think Tiger Lily is our biggest problem. We'll just have to deal with the other things as they come up."

"If that's what you want," said Balo.

Finn nodded his head, and Nissa agreed, too.

"Well, we can't stand around here talking all day. This isn't some picnic," said Balo, his tone sour. He gestured at Lobo. "Well, what are you waiting for?"

Rommy could have sworn she saw the black wolf smile. Did wolves smile? He turned and scanned the forest. Then, glancing over his shoulder, he nodded forward. "We need to go this way," he said. "It will take us along the river. If we make good time, there is a hidden place where we can sleep tonight."

They fell in behind the big wolf, the warrior fairies bringing up the rear. It turned out they had to walk for almost an hour to reach the river. Steep muddy banks hemmed the water in on both sides. Trees stood on raised roots like giant claws tangled in plants and vines.

As they walked, the temperature steadily climbed, and the air got thicker until Rommy felt as if she was being steamed in a giant cooking pot. Finn and Alice were both wiping at their faces with their shirtsleeves. Even the fairies seemed to have dimmed in the heat.

Lobo kept the river within sight, but traveled at a wary distance from the edges where the ground dropped away into the water that frothed and foamed below. While they kept a steady forward pace, it wasn't easy walking. Although the thick plant life had thinned out this deep into the jungle, pillows of moss covered the ground and swelled up from the ground unexpectedly in places. The giant trees rose high above their heads, sheets of moss dripping from their branches. Their roots reached up like fingers through the moist dirt.

Above Rommy's head, the jungle was alive with sounds and movement. Birdsong and squawks mingled with the hum of insects and other noises she couldn't identify. The branches over her head swayed and moved, either with a breeze that didn't reach down to the jungle floor or creatures she couldn't see. She shivered.

Nobody talked much as they walked. Even Balo only muttered an occasional complaint. Alice leaned on Rommy more and more as the day grew warmer and warmer. Even the slight breeze off the river did little to cool them. When Alice had stumbled twice, almost knocking Rommy down the last time, she called to Lobo.

"We need to stop," Rommy said. "It's so warm, maybe we should take a break until it cools off a bit?"

Lobo stopped and backtracked to where they all stood. He nudged his nose against Alice, who looked ready to fall over. Her hair was wet and matted to her head, and her face was red. "You are right," he said. "I am sorry. I am used to walking many miles and forget that you are human and younglings at that." He nodded his head toward a giant tree trunk, its bark shaggy. "We can shelter here for a short time."

They made their way to the tree, which sat where part of the bank jutted out over the river. Alice dropped wearily onto an exposed root and leaned against the trunk of the tree. Rommy handed her the flask of water, and the little girl drank a long swallow.

"Do you have any more of them biscuits?" asked Finn, looking at Rommy hopefully.

She shook her head. "Little Owl gave us what she could, but it's not like she had time to plan. And I lost the sack when Tiger Lily started shooting at us." Rommy turned to Nissa. "Is there something here we can eat and is the water safe to drink?"

Nissa fluttered onto a nearby tree root. "There is cassia fruit close by, and the water here is good. But you will need to go to the water's edge to fill your flask." She made a chittering sound.

Rommy looked doubtfully at the steep riverbank below her. "Trying to find a place where we can fill our flasks might be a problem," she said.

Nissa shook her head. "Yes, it is tricky to find a flat spot, but that isn't the main issue."

Balo buzzed into view. "It's the nixies. Don't you know anything at all?" he shook his head. "It's a wonder you humans weren't killed or died off a long time ago!"

Finn stepped forward. "I'll go fill the flasks," he said. "I've had experience with nixies." He collected the two almost empty flasks from Rommy. As she watched, he collected several leaves and after curling them up, stuffed them into his ears.

"What in the world is he doing?" she asked.

Talen answered without turning from scanning the jungle around them, her tiny spear at the ready. "Nixies lure people into the water with their songs," she said. She made a face. "They are distant cousins of the fairies, but they are nasty creatures."

Balo snorted and flew off. Rommy could hear him muttering something about the "stupid humans," as he went.

Rommy sat down next to Alice and put her arm around the girl. "How are you doing?" she asked.

Alice lifted her chin. "I'm just fine," she said. Then she laughed. "I'd love to see old Danny and his gang stuck out here. He'd be so scared his knees would knock."

Rommy smiled. "I think you're right about that," she said, squeezing Alice's shoulder. "Why don't you rest? It's so warm and we have more walking ahead of us. I might close my eyes, too. We didn't get much sleep last night."

Lobo lay near them on the damp jungle floor, his nose on his front paws. "I will keep watch if you want to rest," he said.

Rommy smiled gratefully, and both girls leaned against the trunk of the tree. It was so wide, they could lean side by side. Alice closed her eyes and was soon asleep. Despite her weariness, though, Rommy found herself wide awake. She looked across at the big, black wolf keeping watch.

Lobo didn't lift his head, but his ears were pricked, and they twitched toward any sound. Rommy watched the large wolf. It was still a mystery to her why he had come with them. After a moment, her curiosity got the better of her.

"Lobo? I've been wondering something," she said. He sat up and tilted his head. She took that as an invitation to continue. "I don't understand why you volunteered to come with us," she said. "I mean, this is dangerous, and don't you miss your pack?"

Lobo considered her question. "I do miss my pack, but I wanted to come with you younglings because it was dangerous."

"But why?" asked Rommy.

"When I was just a cub, one of Peter's boys helped me. I had been stalking a musk rabbit, and a strangler creeper caught me. Before I knew what was happening, it had me tangled in its vines. I thought I wasn't long for the earth."

Rommy leaned forward, caught up in Lobo's story. "How did you get away?"

"Just when I started to lose consciousness, this youngling boy slashed the creeper vines and pulled them off of me," said

Lobo. "He gave me water and revived me. Then he carried me closer to my den before he took off. Helping you and your friends was a way to repay the good done to me." Lobo put his muzzle back on his paws. "This is the reason I've always like humans more than the rest of my pack. You are not all dangerous."

Before Lobo could say anymore, Finn came back juggling several strange-looking hairy fruits and the water flasks. "Hey, I have lunch!" he said.

He squatted down next to Rommy on the giant root and handed her one fruit. She stared at it. "What do I...that is, how do I eat this?"

Finn laughed. "I forgot you've probably never seen one of these." He took the fruit back from her and pulled out a knife from a pocket on his tunic. He expertly sliced it open. Rommy looked at the two glistening halves of the fruit and her stomach lurched. Inside the shaggy shells were whitish gray nubs that looked like maggots. They seemed to be moving. Finn pushed the fruit at her. "Here," he said, "take it. It's good and it will fill you up."

Rommy reached out a hand and gingerly took the fruit from him. He had turned and already sliced open a second fruit. He brought the entire half up to his mouth and took a big bite. Rommy stared at the writhing mass of fruit in her hands. She took a deep breath. In for a penny, in for a pound, as Miss Watson always said. She brought the fruit up to her mouth, and closing her eyes, took a bite. Instead of being sweet, the fruit had a savory taste, which Rommy admitted to herself was good. What was hard to get used to was the moving bits in her mouth, which felt like wiggling worms. Don't think about it, she told herself, chewing.

Alice blinked open sleepy eyes and then, seeing the other slice of fruit in Rommy's hand sat us straight. "Are you eating worms?" she asked, making a face. "I hope you found something else to eat 'cause I ain't eating no worms," she said looking at Finn.

Finn let out a bark of laughter. "These ain't worms," he said, "It's cassia fruit." He held out one half to her. "Here, try it."

Alice wrinkled her nose and shook her head. Finn shook the fruit at her. She stubbornly shook her head again. Rommy could hardly blame her. The fruit really did look like a pile of maggots in a hairy bowl.

Finn bumped Rommy's shoulder. "Tell her how good it tastes," he said.

Rommy looked at Alice. "It really is good," she agreed. "Just close your eyes when you bite into it. That's what I did. It helps."

Alice reluctantly took the fruit that Finn was still holding out to her. She gave Rommy one more questioning look, and when Rommy nodded her head encouragingly, Alice screwed her eyes shut and took a bite. She chewed quickly and swallowed.

"Hey, that's pretty good," she said and then scowled. "If it would only stop moving around in my mouth." She shuddered dramatically.

The fairies gathered around them, watching, and Lobo had lifted his head and was pushing to his feet.

"Can we get going now?" Asked Balo. "Surely you've had enough rest, even for you."

Everyone stood up.

"We should reach a good place to sleep for tonight if we continue until sunset. The little one may ride on my back, if the journey is too much for her." He came to stand in front of Alice and laid down again.

Alice looked at Lobo and then at Rommy. "He said you can ride, Alice, if you'd like to."

"Oh boy, would I!" said Alice, not wasting any time scrambling onto the big black wolf's back. Thus settled, Lobo rose carefully with his burden and set off again. The others fell into step behind him. Rommy wondered just how far Unilisi was into the jungle—and if they'd survive to see her.

Chapter 26:
Beware the Nixies

The group made good time, and just as the jungle darkened, the permanent twilight under the great canopy deepening into darkness, they crested a hillock. As they walked down the other side, the riverbank smoothed out so that the steep banks became only a mild incline to the water's edge. A large tree had fallen there, making a seat of sorts, and a clear space nearby would be a good spot for a fire.

Somewhere along the way, Alice had slumped over asleep, her hands curled into Lobo's fur. The wolf came to a graceful stop without disturbing his passenger.

Rommy walked over and gently shook her shoulder. "Alice, it's time to get down," she said. "We're here."

Alice blinked and sat up. "Where's here?" she asked, rubbing her eyes and looking around.

"We're stopping here for the night," said Finn. He eyed the water. "We need to make sure we aren't too near that river, though."

It didn't take long to set up their camp, such as it was. Finn went with Nissa to collect more food, coming back with not just cassia fruit but also some kind of root. Rommy wasn't sure if she was up for more interesting food.

Talen and Kalen scouted the surrounding jungle and reported that everything seemed secure. Balo gathered vines and plants for a fire, grumbling to himself the entire time. Lobo loped off to hunt for his own dinner.

Darkness had fallen by the time everyone had gathered in the small clearing. Finn had taken the vines and plants that Balo had brought and had a fire going. It turned out the roots were rather tasty once he roasted them over the fire. They reminded Rommy of the roasted potatoes that Chattingham's sometimes served.

Lobo had returned and Alice was leaning against the giant wolf's side, her eyes already heavy. Nissa and Balo made nests for themselves in the branches overhead, and Talen and Kalen said they would take turns guarding the group.

The fire crackled, and for a moment, Rommy relaxed. Sleep tugged at her, but she turned to Finn. In a low voice she asked, "Where do you think Tiger Lily is? Do you think she's followed us?"

Finn shrugged his shoulders. "Tiger Lily is a good tracker, and she's familiar with these jungles. But, it would be pretty stupid to stray off the path on her own. This is a dangerous place for humans, no matter who you are. I think we're safe enough, if we stay off the main trail."

While his words sounded reassuring, Rommy could see his frown in the firelight. "What is it?" she asked. "What's worrying you?"

A look of surprise flashed over Finn's face, but he quickly masked it. "It's just that she knows where we're going," he said. "Moving by herself on the main path, she'll go a lot faster than we can." He shrugged. "At some point we'll end up in the same place to get to Unilisi."

"You think she'll ambush us or something like that?" asked Rommy.

Finn nodded. "It's what I would do, if I was trying to get at someone."

Goosebumps prickled Rommy's skin, and she wrapped her arms around herself to ward off the sudden chill. "What are we going to do? We have to reach Unilisi, and I don't want anything to happen to Alice."

Finn blew out a laugh. "Thanks a lot!"

Rommy shoved his shoulder. "You know I don't want anything to happen to you either, even if you are annoying."

Finn grinned at her. "Yeah, I'm sure your heart'll break if Tiger Lily gets one of her arrows into me." Then his face sobered. "I might have to stay in this jungle since Pan knows where my loyalties lie now."

Rommy put a sympathetic hand on his shoulder. "I'm sorry, Finn," she said, her voice soft. "You saved us, but it's put you into a terrible fix. What will you do? If... when... we get to Unilisi and out of this place? If we can close the passage to Neverland, you can't stay here, can you?"

Finn shrugged again. "That's a lot of ifs," he said. "I think we need to figure out how to keep Tiger Lily from ambushing us first." He jerked a thumb at the wolf who had curled himself around Alice, who was now sleeping. "Lobo should have some ideas, or maybe he'll know a different route to Unilisi that will take us out of Tiger Lily's way."

"I hope so," said Rommy. "I hate to think we'll have big targets on our backs." A yawn caught her by surprise. "I guess we'd better get some sleep."

Finn reached into his pocket and handed her two wads of leaves. "Don't forget to put these in your ears tonight," he said. He nodded toward the water. "The river is full of nixies."

Finn stood and offered Rommy his hand. She took it, and he pulled her to her feet. Rommy looked up at him.

"I was wrong before," she said. "You aren't a coward at all. You're rather brave." Before she could think better of it, she rose on her toes and kissed his cheek.

Her face flaming, she didn't even look at him. Instead, she quickly stepped over to where Alice was sleeping on the opposite side of the fire and dropped down next to her. She squeezed her eyes shut, the leaves forgotten in her hand.

Lilting music. It floated through her dreams, pulling her toward wakefulness. Rommy blinked open her eyes. She could still hear the music, and oh the moonlight. It was so beautiful, reflecting off the water. It seemed to call her.

Carefully, Rommy disentangled herself from Alice and padded softly toward the water's edge. The mud squished under her boots, but she had to get closer. The pool shimmered in the moonlight, and the music seemed to beckon her.

She knelt on the edge of the bank and looked into the shining depths of the placid river. A beautiful face looked back her. Waves of hair as green as grass floated around a face with large silvery eyes that seemed liquid. The mouth was open in a song that harmonized with the stars' melody overhead.

Something nagged at the back of Rommy's mind, but she pushed it away impatiently. She had to get closer to the music. She leaned farther over the gently flowing water.

The creature lifted a hand from what looked like the other side of a mirror. Again, something poked at the back of Rommy's mind. Her hand hovered in mid-air and she hesitated. The music pushed into her mind, and whatever had been trying to get her attention drifted away.

She reached out and her hand skimmed the surface of the water. For a moment, her palm touched that of the water creature's, and she smiled. The creature smiled back.

Suddenly, bony fingers wrapped around her wrist, and she was being pulled. The creature's face broke the water, but it wasn't beautiful anymore. The green hair hung like slimy ropes of seaweed, and the mouth was filled with sharp teeth Rommy hadn't noticed before. The beautiful music of a moment before turned into an earsplitting screech that sounded like chalk on a blackboard.

Rommy pulled back, trying to tug her hand away from the creature's grip, but the bony fingers were like iron bands on her wrist. Rommy shrieked as she felt herself being yanked toward the water. Finn's warning about nixies flashed through her mind, and terror pooled in her stomach.

She strained back, and her feet dug into the loose, rocky soil, trying to find purchase, but the nixie kept pulling her forward. Rommy skidded into the shallows of the water, and she scrabbled around with her other hand, trying to find a vine or anything to hold on to.

Then her shirt was gripped from behind, her wrist was ripped from the creature's hand, and she was being pulled from the edge. Her breath came fast and her whole body shook. A low growl sounded next to her. The nixie gave a last screech, and with a flip of her scaly tail, disappeared beneath the water, a v-like wake following her retreat.

"Rommy, are you okay?" Finn was beside her, helping her to her feet. Her legs felt loose and watery, like all the strength had drained from them. She shook her head, still dazed.

"What...what happened?" she said, her voice trembling.

"It was one of those dratted nixies," said Finn. "Didn't you stuff those leaves in your ears?"

Heat crawled up her neck and she glanced away. "I...I completely forgot."

"That ugly thing was a nixie?" asked Alice, walking up beside them, yawning. "Didn't you think it was scary?"

Rommy shook her head. "No, when it was singing, it looked beautiful and kind." A shudder rippled through her again at how close the thing had come to pulling her into the river.

Lobo scanned the water once more before returning to her side. "They are very predatory," he said. "You are fortunate Finn and I woke up. Once they have ahold of someone, not many humans live to tell the tale."

By this time, the fairies had all awoken and were hovering around. Balo came to a stop in front of Rommy's face. He shoved two green wads at her. "Here, girl," he said. "Put these in your ears, unless you want to become a nixie meal." He harrumphed loudly when Rommy tried to thank him. "Just stuff them in your ears so I can get some sleep." He flew back to his nest in the trees.

The rest of them made their way back to the fallen tree. It took a while for everyone to settle back in their places. Rommy stuffed the green wads in her ears and made sure Alice's were firmly in place, too. She didn't know if the nixie would try again, but she wasn't chancing it.

It didn't take too long for the others to fall back to sleep, despite all the drama, but Rommy found herself staring up at the lavender moon. When she closed her eyes, the nixie's face loomed in her mind. She couldn't help the shudder that rippled over her when she remembered the creature's cold, bony fingers around her wrist. A few faint dark smudges on her wrist showed in the moonlight. Bruises. If that creature had succeeded, she would have never seen her papa again. Their last words would have been angry. Tears pricked behind her eyes, and she felt a pang of guilt. Rommy just hoped their journey was successful so that she could explain to Papa why she had left.

Chapter 27: Almost There

Someone was nudging her shoulder. Rommy tried to push the person away and felt fur. She blinked into the dim morning light and sat up. Lobo's blue eyes stared into hers before he stepped back. Everything sounded muffled, and it took a moment before she remembered the leaves stuffed into her ears. She pulled them out and the sounds of the jungle rushed in. The birds made a loud clamor in the surrounding trees.

Rommy got to her feet and absently rubbed her wrist. When she looked down, there was a bracelet of bruises around it. Dumb nixie, she thought with a frown.

Alice shoved half of a cassia fruit into her hands. "Eat up," she said. "We gotta move it."

Finn was finishing his fruit, and the fairies were fluttering around the camp. Lobo was sitting on his haunches, waiting for them all, his ears pricked forward.

Rommy popped the last bite of fruit into her mouth and wiped her hands on her pants. She was almost used to the way the cassia fruit wiggled in her mouth now. Almost.

She looked at Lobo. "Do you think we'll find Unilisi today?" she asked.

He shook his shaggy black head. "No, we probably have another day's journey. If we travel quickly, we may reach the center of the jungle by sunset."

Rommy looked over at Finn, who nodded at her. "Lobo, do you know a different way to Unilisi?" she asked. "Tiger Lily can travel much faster than we can, and she could reach the Unilisi's grove before we do."

Lobo's muzzle wrinkled. "We can circle around, but if she is watching for us, I do not know how to avoid her. There is only one way to Unilisi."

Rommy sighed, her shoulders slumping. "I guess we will have to figure out a plan, then. Now, though, we should get started."

Lobo tilted his head. "A pack is stronger than a lone wolf," he said.

Rommy patted his side. "You are right."

Lobo headed back into the jungle, and the rest of the group fell into a familiar formation. Rommy followed Lobo with Alice close beside her. Finn brought up the rear with Nissa zipping around him. Talen and Kalen ranged behind them, keeping a lookout. Balo buzzed up and down the line, mostly complaining that they weren't going fast enough.

The day passed much as the previous one had, minus being shot at, of course. As the sun climbed in the sky, so did the temperature. While the heavy canopy of trees blocked the direct rays of the sun, it also made the breezes sparse. The humidity settled over them like a wet blanket. Insects buzzed around Rommy's head, and sweat dripped down her face and back. She looked at the river that ran along the path with longing, but memories of the nixie kept her far away from its banks.

The small band of travelers took a short break for lunch and then continued on their way, this time with Alice perched on Lobo's back.

As the sun slanted with the afternoon light, Rommy noticed that the jungle floor was climbing gradually but steadily. The huge pillows of moss were interrupted with large boulders and rocks that became more frequent the longer they walked. The plants grew thicker and the trees thinned out the higher they went.

Eventually, Lobo came to a stop and faced them. "If we continue straight on, we will come to the grove of Unilisi, which is at the top. We can only enter there at dawn. We should circle around the backside of the grove and camp there."

Finn rubbed the back of his neck. "I think Lobo has the right idea. If we go around the back, we shouldn't run into Tiger Lily. It will give us time to come up with a plan."

Rommy nodded in agreement.

"I don't care what we do as long as we eat soon," said Alice from Lobo's back. "I'm so hungry my ribs is talking to my back."

Rommy grinned at the little girl. Lobo, seeing they were in agreement, turned and walked downhill, and they all followed. It took almost an hour for the group to hike to the small clearing where Lobo led them to rest for the night.

The clearing was ringed by thin, flexible trees topped with balls of fuzzy leaves in shades of yellow and orange. Vines with purple stripes hung from some branches and swayed, despite the lack of breeze. Rommy felt a sense of unease but brushed it away. They were almost there. Tomorrow they would see Unilisi. She would help them. Rommy wouldn't allow herself to think of any other outcome, not after all they had been through.

Chapter 28:
Deadly Flora

Rommy stretched her legs out in front of her and wiggled her toes. She had pulled off her boots to ease the ache in her feet. After tramping through the jungle for two days, her whole body was weary, and she felt sticky and in need of a good bath. She glanced over at Alice. Despite the long journey, the little girl's eyes were bright as she teased with Finn.

A movement out of the corner of her eye caught Rommy's attention. She looked toward the nearest tree. Was it her imagination, or did that vine seem closer? She shook her head. Now she was seeing things. She took another bite of a root that Finn had scavenged. He had also found cloudberries. She popped one in her mouth, and the bright pink orbs burst over her tongue in a rush of sweetness.

A creak made her turn her head again. This time she knew she wasn't imagining things. The vine that had been hanging from one of the nearby fuzzy-topped trees only a few minutes ago now lay on the ground.

"Um, Finn? Lobo?" she said, her eyes darting to the other trees and noting that their vines all seemed to have moved closer, too.

Finn looked up, still smiling from something Alice was saying. "What's wrong?" he asked.

Rommy pointed. "Those vines," she said. "They're moving toward us. Should we be worried about that?"

Finn leaped to his feet, and Lobo pushed to his. They both swung around to face the trees, and the vines slithered forward.

"Those are Viper Vines," said Lobo. "But they rarely attack unless someone awakens them."

"Well, what did we do to awaken them?" asked Rommy.

"And how do we make 'em go back to sleep?" said Alice, taking a step closer to Rommy.

"They don't sleep again until they've fed," said Finn, staring at one vine that was moving forward more quickly than the others.

"What do they eat?" asked Rommy.

Finn swallowed. "Whatever they can find."

"Well, they sure ain't finding me," said Alice. "We need to bunk it before these slithering things get us." She took a step toward a gap in the trees, but Finn clamped his hand on her shoulder.

"No, Alice, don't run," he said. "That will just make it worse."

Alice crossed her arms. "Worse? How can it be worse? What are we supposed to do? Just stand here and let 'em eat one of us? I'm not volunteering, that's for sure."

Lobo watched the vines, a low growl rumbling deep in his throat.

"Well, how do we stop them?" asked Rommy, panic forming a lump in her chest as the vines kept moving closer.

"We convince them we aren't easy prey," said Finn, pulling his dagger from his belt.

Rommy drew the knife Little Owl had given her from its sheath.

"They do not like fire, either," said Lobo and clamped one of the sticks from the fire between his teeth.

Alice grabbed another burning stick and waved it at the nearest vine, which had crept almost to her foot. It drew back, writhing on the ground.

Rommy stabbed down at another vine, and Finn did the same. Soon, the vines had all drawn back, but it was only temporary. After just a moment or two, they crept forward again.

Balo flew over a vine and rubbed his small hands together. When he pulled them apart, a glowing ball hovered between them. He brought it up to his mouth, whispered something, and then blew on it. The sphere rocketed toward the vine, hitting it and causing a stream of smoke. Rommy heard a hissing noise.

"Is...is that vine hissing?" she asked.

Finn raised an eyebrow. "It *is* a Viper Vine," he said, just before he stabbed at another one that had flopped against his foot.

Rommy, Alice, Finn, and Lobo stood facing outward in a tight circle. By stabbing and waving the fire at the vines, they were able to keep them from creeping too close. But Rommy knew they were going to have to find a way to stop them permanently. They couldn't do this indefinitely.

Between thwacking any creeping green thing that got too close, she called over her shoulder, "When will they give up?"

"Not until they feed," was Finn's grim reply.

"Not ever?" Alice asked, waving her torch at a slender shoot that had curled around her foot.

"Not unless we kill 'em," said Finn. "And you hafta cut them off from the root."

Balo and the other fairies continued to blow their glowing orbs at the vines, which made them smoke and hiss but didn't seem to cause permanent damage.

"Balo," said Rommy, "can you get to the root of these things?"

Balo scowled. "Not easily," he said. "They're not going to just let me waltz right up to their root and cut them off."

Kalen and Talen buzzed around to face Rommy. "We will help find the root," said Talen. Kalen nodded his head in agreement. Rommy wasn't sure if she had ever heard the dark-haired fairy speak. His sister always seemed to speak for both of them.

"Can you do it without getting attacked?" she said.

Talen put her small fist over her chest. "We have sworn to protect you, and we will kill the Viper Vines even if we give up our own lives."

Rommy opened her mouth to speak, but the two fairies were already gone. She pressed her lips together. She would not let anyone in this group die if she could help it. Gripping her knife, she slashed at the vines with renewed energy.

Two of the vines slithered away from the group. Rommy smiled in triumph. The plan was working.

Suddenly a scream ripped through the air.

Rommy whipped her head in the direction from which the sound had come. She could make out a form struggling wildly behind one of the thin, whip-like trees. She and Finn looked at each other. He pressed his lips in a tight line.

Two vines had left, having found new prey. Two others were thrashing on the ground. While Rommy looked on, they went limp. That left two more vines that were still insistently creeping toward the group, but their odds had improved.

Another scream sounded, fainter than before, and without even fully deciding, Rommy was running toward the struggling form.

"Wait," said Finn, but Rommy ignored him.

She burst through the ring of trees into the jungle. A dark head was visible, but the vines had twisted up the person's body. The one arm that wasn't wrapped in the green leaves was trying to fight off the vines, but it was clear it was a losing battle.

The plant tangled into a long dark braid, pulling the person's head back. The vines twisted tighter, and the person gasped for breath. Rommy's hazel eyes met fierce black ones.

The eyes narrowed when they met Rommy's.

"You," the girl said, almost spitting the word.

It was Tiger Lily.

Chapter 29:
To Save Your Enemy

For a moment, Rommy hesitated, the knife gripped in her hand. Then she shook her head, appalled at herself that the idea of leaving Tiger Lily to her fate had even crossed her mind. What was happening to her in this crazy place?

Without a word, Rommy lifted her knife, and the other girl closed her eyes. They popped back open as Rommy slashed at the vines twisting around Tiger Lily. It seemed to take forever, but finally, the vines dropped away, slithering off her and leaving stray leaves on the other girl's clothes and hair.

Tiger Lily swayed on her feet, and Rommy put her arm around the other girl's waist. "We should move away from those things," she said, nodding at the vines that still writhed on the ground. "They'll probably try again."

Rommy helped the older, taller girl limp to a nearby rock, where Tiger Lily sat, her legs giving way. She sat still, breathing deeply for several moments. Finally, she looked up at Rommy.

"Why did you help me, your enemy?" Tiger Lily asked, a frown creasing her forehead.

Rommy shrugged. "I couldn't just let you die," she said.

"But why?" Tiger Lily persisted.

Rommy blew her hair out of her face. "Because you simply don't do that, that's why. Just be glad my conscience is more active than yours."

Tiger Lily looked down at her hands that were clenched into trembling fists. "But I woke the vines," she said. "I would have let them kill you, but you saved me."

Rommy lifted an eyebrow. "You know, you should probably stop reminding me of that. Even though I didn't let those vines choke you, we haven't decided what we should do with you yet, either."

Tiger Lily opened her hands and held them out to Rommy. "I failed," she said. "You should have let the vines take me."

Rommy sighed, a deep weariness settling on her shoulders. "I don't understand why you are doing this, Tiger Lily," she said. "You may hate my father, and I'm his daughter. But Alice and Finn have done nothing to you. Why would you try to kill them?"

A long silence stretched out, but just when Rommy thought the girl would not say anything at all, she spoke. "You do not understand. I had to help Peter," she said. Her eyes pierced Rommy's. "He needs me. I love him, and he loves me. He's all I have."

Rommy shook her head. "I don't believe he loves anyone," she said. "And you have your family. They love you, and I'm sure they're worried about you."

Tiger Lily's eyes snapped with anger. "What do you know of love?" she said. "You are still a little girl tied to her worthless father."

Rommy felt her own anger spurt. This hateful girl had caused no end of trouble for her, and she had hurt Alice more than once. Not to mention, they could have all died from those nasty vines.

"I may be younger than you are, but even I know people who love you try to protect you. They don't put you in danger," she said. She leaned forward and stared into Tiger Lily's face. "I know that if Pan truly loves you, he wouldn't risk your life, sending you to go do his dirty work. He's using you, and you're too blind to see it."

Tiger Lily pushed to her feet. Rommy thrust her arm forward until her knife was an inch away from the other girl's chest. Something tickled her foot, and she looked down. The last vine had slithered closer again, and Rommy quickly sliced at it. Tiger Lily, using the moment of distraction, shoved away from her.

"Hey," yelled Rommy, but the girl had recovered more quickly than Rommy realized. Within a moment, the taller girl was several yards away.

Tiger Lily paused on top of a fallen tree and looked back at Rommy. Her face was pale as her eyes met Rommy's and locked there. "I am in your debt," she said. "I give you my word. I will not try to harm you or your friends again until I pay it."

Before Rommy could respond, Tiger Lily darted away. Finn came jogging up beside her while Rommy still stared at where Tiger Lily had been.

"Hey, what happened?" he asked. "I heard you yell. Are you all right?" He nudged the vine, which was now limp on the ground.

"Yes, but I lost Tiger Lily," said Rommy.

"Tiger Lily? You mean she was the one screaming?" He rolled his eyes. "I should have guessed."

Rommy nodded. "She's the one who woke those vines, but they turned on her. I sliced her loose, but before I could call anyone over, that vine started moving. When I stabbed it, she got away."

Finn rubbed both hands on the top of his head, making his shaggy hair stand up on end. "What are we going to do about her? She knows where we are now."

"She said she was in my debt and won't harm us," said Rommy, shrugging, "but I don't know how much we can trust her word. She's besotted with Pan. That's why she was here, to help him."

Finn frowned. "A debt of honor is something Tiger Lily and her people take very seriously," he said. "I expect she won't try to hurt us again, but that doesn't mean she won't tell Pan where we are."

They walked back over to the others. All the vines were lying limp and unmoving on the ground now. Alice perched on a stump with Nissa hovering near her. Lobo was sitting on his haunches, ears pricked forward.

When Rommy and Finn entered the clearing, Lobo whined. He walked over to her and gently laid his muzzle on her shoulder. Rommy leaned her head against his for a moment, burying her fingers in his thick fur. Just for a moment, she let his strength flow into her.

Finally, taking a deep breath, she told the others what had happened. "Tiger Lily ran away, but she feels she owes me a debt, so I think we can trust she won't try to harm us again."

Finn added, "She'll probably tell Pan, but she has to get out of the jungle first. We should be able to reach Unilisi before that happens."

Balo made a snorting sound. "I can't believe you saved her," he complained. "After I risk my life killing those vines, you let her go so that she can tell Pan right where we are? Sometimes, I think you enjoy almost dying."

Nissa hissed. "Balo, you weren't the only one who was killing the vines." She had her hands on her tiny hips, and the glow around her was taking on a brighter hue. "Now, stop complaining. We must prepare for Unilisi tomorrow, and it is already late."

Rommy felt a flutter in her stomach. "You're right, Nissa," she said. "We need to gather the items Little Owl told us to, and we need to leave at first light. She said the best time to pass the guardian trees into Unilisi's grove is when dawn is just breaking."

Nissa called over Balo, and the two of them flew off to gather the special blossoms they would need. Rommy gathered the leaves of the fuzzy trees and then looked at Finn. "Do you have any idea how to make these into a basket?" she asked, staring at them.

He chuckled. "Didn't they teach you basket weaving in that fancy school of yours?" he asked, his eyes twinkling.

Rommy laughed. "No, that's one thing we never learned."

Alice came to squat next to them. Finn went over to one of the thin trees, and using his knife, made a score along the trunk. A thin line of sap oozed out. He scraped it off and then smeared it on the leaves, building them up until they formed a little cup-like basket.

It didn't take long before Nissa and Balo returned with yellow and white blossoms. "Balo, go kill the vines. Balo, go get the flowers. Balo, do this. Balo, do that," the auburn-haired fairy grumbled. "Nobody even says thank you."

Rommy bit back a smile, stood, and walked over to where he perched on a low branch. Dropping a kiss on his tiny head, she said, "Thank you, Balo. You've been a big help on this trip, and I, for one, appreciate it."

He crossed his arms and huffed, but Rommy thought she saw him starting to smile when he turned away.

Finn had found a few branches and leaves and started a small fire. The others gathered around it. The long day's journey plus the encounter with the deadly vines had exhausted everyone.

"We should get some rest," Rommy said. "We'll need to start out early."

Everyone settled down to sleep, although Rommy saw Alice look over at the vines several times before her eyes drifted shut. She hoped the girl didn't have nightmares. For that matter, she hoped she didn't have nightmares. Between this and all the times she'd almost died in the past week, she had a lot of material for them. Her last thought as her eyes fluttered shut was that she hoped this trip hadn't been for nothing.

Chapter 30:
Meeting Unilisi

The jungle was still dark when the small group got ready to leave their campsite. The shadowy outlines of the Viper Vines lay motionless and limp on the ground, their stripes faded to nothing.

Rommy saw Alice make a wide circle around one as they headed back out of the clearing. Lobo once again led them with Rommy behind him. The fairies spread out, Kalen up with Lobo and Talen bringing up the rear behind Finn.

Nissa flew next to Rommy, humming as she went. Balo had flittered further away, his golden glow barely visible.

Lobo set a brisk pace, as they needed to be at Unilisi's grove at dawn. The nerves that in Rommy's stomach churned. She hadn't even tried to eat one of the cassia fruits that Finn had gathered for her and Alice.

Questions seemed to repeat themselves in time to her steps. What if Unilisi wouldn't talk to them? What if they didn't even get past the guardian trees? Little Owl had explained the words Rommy was supposed to say so that the trees would allow the group into the grove. The elderly woman had warned her that sometimes, the trees blocked people's path for reasons of their own. And trying to get by a guardian tree was unwise and often fatal.

At the time, Rommy had wondered what a tree could do to a person, but after the Viper Vines, she decided she didn't want to find out.

As the path slanted upward, Rommy panted with the effort. The slope wasn't steep, but the ground had gotten rockier and more overgrown as they got closer to open sky, making walking more difficult. Alice stumbled against her, and Rommy put out a hand to steady her.

"Are you okay?" she asked the younger girl.

"I'm fine and dandy," said Alice, although her words came between puffs of breath.

Lobo stopped and looked back. "I do not mean to push so hard, but the sun will welcome the day soon," he said. "Perhaps you should ride."

Alice didn't need to be asked twice. She scurried past Rommy and clambered onto Lobo's back, where she patted the big wolf on his neck. "You are the best wolf I've ever met," she said, then grinned. "Course, I ain't met too many wolves."

Lobo trotted on, and Rommy hurried to keep up. It wouldn't be long now. The ground became increasingly difficult to navigate. Over last several yards, Rommy scrabbled up a steep incline onto a flat plateau. After looking around, she realized they were on the top of a small hill that rose out of the surrounding jungle. The tangle of plants and vines grew right up to a thick ring of trees that encircled the center of the hilltop.

It was Unilisi's grove.

Rommy's heart hammered in her chest so loudly she was surprised none of the others could hear it. This was it. Their quest could be over or just starting.

Alice slipped off Lobo, and Finn came to stand next to her as the first rays of the sun peeked through the trees.

"Do you remember the words?" asked Nissa.

Rommy nodded. Finn reached over and squeezed her hand. She gave him a grateful smile and her lips trembled.

She pressed them together and lifted her chin. She hadn't come this far to let a few nerves stop her. Squaring her shoulders, she walked toward the ring of trees. When she got about six feet from them, the branches swung down to block her way. As the first rays of dawn stretched over the grove, the leaves glinted gold and silver, their edges gleaming with knife-like sharpness. No wonder Little Owl said it was impossible to get by unless the guardian trees allowed it.

Rommy closed the distance between herself and the trees and stood before the branches that blocked the entrance. She brought Little Owl's words into her mind, took a deep breath, and then spoke.

Guardians of Unilisi
I ask for entrance
For my friends and me
We have come from a great distance
To seek the great grandmother of us all
Without her wisdom, we will fall.

Rommy held her breath. After a long agonizing moment there was creaking and groaning, and the branches pulled back, making an entrance. Rommy gestured to the others, and they hurried over. The opening only allowed one person at a time, and Rommy was the first to step into the grove. As soon as both her feet were inside the circle, the trees snapped shut behind her.

"Hey!" Alice shouted from the other side. "Let us in, you stupid trees!"

The branches didn't move. Uneasiness made a cold trail up Rommy's spine. Little Owl had said nothing about having to do this alone.

Rommy pushed away her unease and looked around. Inside the ring of trees was a small clearing. Green grass dotted with a rainbow of wildflowers carpeted the ground. The blossoms nodded in an invisible breeze and let out the soft tinkle of tiny bells. Butterflies of every color shimmered through the air.

She caught her breath as a brilliant turquoise butterfly the size of a bird alighted on her shoulder. It fanned its delicate wings a few times before flitting off.

In the center of the clearing stood a large tree, its trunk bigger than anything Rommy had ever seen. The roots at its base were visible, hunched up and gnarled, before disappearing into the ground. Its branches spread so wide and leafy that they almost capped the entire clearing. The tree gave off its own glow, and the sun filtered through the leaves, making each one shimmer like silver charms.

Rommy stood gaping for a moment and then remembered what she needed to do. She gently gripped the little leaf cup with the blossoms and walked toward the tree. Each step she took stirred up butterflies and made the wildflowers chime madly.

As she drew closer, she found it harder and harder to move forward. The air around the great tree seemed thick and pulsing. She felt her mind going fuzzy at the edges, and she had to wrench her thoughts to what she needed to do next.

She placed the cup with its blossoms at the heart of a big root. Then she went down on one knee, placing her fist against her shoulder and bowing her head, as Little Owl had instructed her.

And then she waited.

And waited.

The butterflies continued to flit over the flowers, some alighting on her hair and shoulders. The wildflowers swayed and tinkled.

And still she waited.

Just when she wondered if she should try to leave, a great heaving sigh breathed out of the tree, and the leaves rustled and clinked. She felt the pulsing thickness press on her head, and then it lessened.

There came a deep sigh. "Ah, another day, another pilgrim comes to get answers. Stand up and tell me why you are here." The voice was raspy and impatient.

Rommy scrambled to her feet, blinking in surprise. Where gnarled tree bark had been, she could see a face, like an ancient grandmother.

Rommy swallowed. "I have come to you for answers, Unil-isi."

The eyes in the tree bark seemed to roll. "Well, I didn't think you came to have a picnic. You'll have to be more specific. What answers do you need?

"Oh, well, I..." said Rommy, startled by the tree's abrupt tone.

"Speak up, speak up," said the tree. "What? Do you think I have all the time in the world?" It paused and then cackled, a sound like dry leaves being crushed. "Well, as to that, I guess I do, don't I?" After several moments, it sputtered to a stop and spoke again. "Regardless, I certainly don't have all the time in the world for you. The clock is ticking, Child, so I suggest you spit out that question before I lose my patience all together."

Rommy cleared her throat and gathered her thoughts. This was not going the way she had imagined. "I need to know how to close the passage from Neverland to the outside world."

"Humph! And why do you need to know that? That passage has been open a long time, and there's been no problem. Why do you want to close it now?"

"Peter Pan is kidnapping children," said Rommy. "He is taking them from their beds against their will."

"You do not have to describe what kidnapping is," the tree said. "I've been around long enough to know what that means. And how does this concern me, exactly?"

Rommy was starting to feel exasperated. She took another deep breath to calm herself. "If we can close that passageway, then Peter Pan can no longer take anyone." Again, she felt a pressure in her head like the tree was rummaging around in her mind.

"Is that really the reason you want to close off the passageway?" Unilisi said, one gnarled eyebrow rising.

"Isn't that enough of a reason?" Rommy asked.

The other eyebrow joined its mate.

Rommy sighed and kicked at the dirt. Her words came in a rush. "I want my father back. Pan took my brother, and he died here. My father wants revenge so much, it's making him into someone I don't know, and...sometimes, I don't like, either."

The tree rustled and creaked. "Ah, now we get to the heart of the matter. Everyone wants to act as if they are about some noble cause, but usually, at the root of it all is a heart's desire. You want your father to be your father."

Rommy wrinkled her nose.

Again, the tree sighed. "Must I explain everything to you? You want your father to do his job, to be *your* father, not your brother's father. After all, your brother doesn't need your father anymore, and you do."

Rommy's eyes opened wide and then narrowed. "That's exactly how I feel. How did you know that?"

The tree made a tsking sound. "You traveled all this way to visit an ancient, wise being, and now you are asking me why I know things? I thought if you were smart enough to get here, you would catch onto things more quickly."

Heat crawled up Rommy's neck, and she wished she could suck back her words.

"Oh, don't look like that," Unilisi said and sighed again. "I'm sure you are a bright enough girl. I will tell you what you want to know, but first, you must understand, if the passage is closed, it can never be opened again."

"That's not a problem," said Rommy. "Once it's closed with Pan here, there is no reason to open it again."

"Once you start the process, you will only have from sunrise to sunrise before the passageway is sealed," said Unilisi. "Anyone who is still on this island will stay here. Forever. Once the locking is set into motion, it cannot be stopped, not even by me. Are you willing to take that chance?"

Rommy swallowed and then nodded.

The tree paused and then rustled its branches. Several small black berries dropped at Rommy's feet. "There is another way," said the tree. "Those berries at your feet are poisonous. One bite and they kill instantly."

Rommy looked into the ancient bark face, unwilling to say aloud what she thought the tree was trying to tell her. Unilisi rustled her branches again and let out a huff.

"Don't give me that innocent look," she said. "You know I'm referring to Peter Pan. Those berries would get rid of him and be safer for you and your friends. No danger of being sealed forever on Neverland, and no need to worry about Pan anymore. Your father would have his revenge, and you'd have your father. It's a simple solution."

Rommy sucked in a breath and quickly stepped back from the berries. "I...I couldn't do that," she said. "What Pan is doing is wrong, and I want nothing more for my father to leave this place. But...I could never...kill Pan. That would be just as wrong as what he's been doing."

The tree cackled again, and a shower of silvery leaves fell on Rommy's head. "I knew you had some nobleness in there, even if it is mixed up with your longings," Unilisi said. "Besides, I haven't had any visitors in a long time. It will be interesting to help you and see what happens. Step closer."

Rommy let out a long breath. She moved closer to the ancient tree, and a wave of power washed over her. A picture of what looked like a glowing dark green stick formed in Rommy's mind. It was nestled in a tangled bird's nest. Unilisi's voice echoed inside her head.

"You must find the key to Neverland in the home of the fairy who opened the gate, but beware. Her anchor of hope has come unmoored." The picture wavered and changed to an underwater cave, where a tall stone door stood between two stone pillars. In the center of the door was a round opening. "Then you must go to the Cave of Sighs that is guarded by the mermaid princesses and put the key into the lock. Turn it three times, and the passageway will start to close. Everyone who wants to leave must do so between the next two sunrises. Anyone still on the island when the rays of the second sunrise touch the rock in the center of Mermaid Lagoon will be sealed here forever. Do you understand?"

Rommy nodded. "But where is the key?" she asked. "Who was the fairy who opened the gate?"

But Unilisi had gone silent. The trunk was only bark once more. Rommy heard rustling, and several silvery leaves fluttered down to her feet.

"Each of these leaves are wishes for you, but use them wisely," Unilisi's voice echoed. "Now go while the Guardians will let you."

Rommy put her hand on the trunk of the tree. "Thank you," she said.

The tree rustled again. The voice floated into her head. "Enough of that. Now go. Shoo, I say."

Rommy picked up the leaves and turned toward the ring of trees. Two had swung up their branches, and there was a narrow opening into the jungle outside. She ran toward it and her friends who were waiting outside the circle of trees, Unilisi's silver leaves clenched in her hand.

Chapter 31:
Not Another Quest

When Rommy broke through the ring of trees, Alice nearly barreled her over.

"Are you all right? What happened? Was that tree person a right git?" Alice's questions tumbled over each other.

Rommy let out a laugh. "Slow down, Alice, and I'll tell you all about it, but let me get my breath first."

Finn and Lobo had joined them and were looking at her with expectant faces. The fairies flickered around all of them. Rommy walked away from the Guardian trees. It seemed somehow rude to talk about Unilisi when they were standing so close to her grove.

When they had walked a short distance away, Rommy stopped and looked at them. "Unilisi wasn't what I expected," she said, "but she told me what we need to do to close the passage."

Rommy explained about finding the key and the lock, and about the amount of time they'd have to get everyone out of Neverland who wanted to go.

"When I asked who the fairy was that opened the gate and how to find her, she never answered me," Rommy finished. "Little Owl said a fairy named Tinkerbell was the one that pleaded for Pan to come here. Where would we find her?" she asked, looking at Finn.

Finn rubbed the back of his neck. "I'm not exactly sure," he said. "I've heard that name, from Pan and some of the fairies, but I've never seen her."

At the name, Balo muttered a word Rommy didn't recognize but guessed it wasn't very nice by Nissa's reaction.

"Balo!" she scolded. Turning to Rommy, Nissa's face looked solemn. "Nobody has seen Tinkerbell in a long, long time. She has exiled herself from the fairy colony." She paused and then said, "Fairies do not do well on their own. If she is still alive, she will not be...well."

"Do you mean, she's...crazy?" Rommy asked. "Why would she exile herself if it would make her crazy?"

"Nobody knows. She was a close companion to Peter for many years," said Nissa, "but then three humans came to the island, a girl and two boys. I never learned what happened, but it was shortly after they left that Tinkerbell disappeared. Nobody knows where she is, or even if she is still alive."

"Unilisi showed me a picture in my head of the key in what looked like a very large, messy bird's nest," said Rommy. "I didn't see a fairy, though."

Balo harrumphed. "Sounds like a fairy nest to me," he said. He threw up his hands and buzzed in a tight circle. "That's just wonderful! Now we need to go looking for a crazy, feral fairy! Traveling through the jungle and almost getting killed half a dozen times was bad enough."

Rommy could see Nissa rolling her eyes. Kalen and Talen, as usual, were not participating in the conversation. Instead, they faced outward, scanning the surroundings for signs of trouble.

"Even if we find this key, trying to get into somewhere that the mermaids are guarding won't be easy," said Finn. "Step one foot into that water, and Adela and Arista will try to drown you, never mind trying to swim down to some cave. How will we even find it?"

"The redheaded mermaid might help us," said Rommy. "She's the one that cut me loose when Pan tied me to that rock."

Finn was already shaking his head. "She seems the nicest of the lot, but you can't trust any of the mermaids, not really. I wouldn't count on her helping you again."

Rommy threw up her hands. "I didn't come all this way and get answers from Unilisi just so that everyone can tell me what we can't do," she said. "As far as I can see it, there is no choice. If we don't close the passageway, what are you going to do, Finn? You can't go back to the Lost Boys now. Pan will be hunting you."

Finn scowled. "You don't have to tell me that I'll be in Pan's crosshairs, but *you* can leave. Take your father and go back to London."

"Don't you think I would if I could?" she shot back. "Even if my father would go—which he won't—I can't just waltz back to London like I'm unaware Pan is kidnapping children or that you're in danger now." Her voice wobbled, so she sucked in a deep breath. Then she said in a low voice, "I thought you knew me better than that."

Finn kicked at the dirt. "You don't belong here, Rommy, or you either, Alice. This isn't even your problem. I should have never brought either of you here."

"Well, you did," Rommy said, her voice rising. "And I can't just act like I never learned all this. I can't understand why you'd expect, after all this that I'd just leave."

Anger bubbled up, threatening to overflow. She whirled and walked away. Before she had gotten too far, Finn grabbed her arm.

"You sure have your old man's temper," he said when she was facing him again. Rommy opened her mouth, but he held up his hand. "I'm sorry," he said. "I know you probably figure I'm always the one pointing out all the problems, but I guess I've gotten used to looking for trouble."

He folded his arms and looked out into the wildness all around them. "The thing is, Rommy, I've lost count how many times you've about got yourself killed since I brought you here. Even though you have a knack for finding your way out of trouble, one of these days your luck will run out." He blew out a breath. "I know we've gotta stop Pan, and we're the ones to do it. But I wish...I wish...that is, I'm the one that brought you here. If it hadn't been for me, you'd be tucked up safe in that boarding school of yours."

Rommy sighed, her anger leaking away. "But I don't *want* to be tucked up anywhere," she said. "Do you think I *want* to do this impossible thing? I'm no more eager to swim with murderous mermaids than you are." She paused, looking for the right words. "But, sometimes, it's more important to recognize the truth and be able to do something about it than to just be comfortable and safe. I spent most of my life being comfortable and safe, but it was all really a lie. If I ran back to London now, it would be like I'm still living that lie. I can't do that anymore."

Finn gave a half smile. "I see you can't." He ran a hand through his hair, making it stand up on end. "I can't promise I won't point out trouble, but I will help you."

Rommy looked up at him and felt a foolishly large grin spread across her face. He looked into her eyes and smiled back.

"If you two is finished jawin' at each other, maybe we can get a move on?" Alice said, pushing her way between the two. "I don't want to spend any more time in this here jungle than I have to. I've almost died way too many times already!"

Finn and Rommy both burst out laughing. She dropped her arm around the younger girl's shoulders. "You're right, Alice," she said, wiping at her eyes, "the sooner we get out of here, the sooner we can try to find that key and close the passage."

Chapter 32:
Out of the Jungle,
Into the Frying Pan

It took a whole day and much of the next for the group to make its way out of the jungle. Rommy made sure everyone stuffed their ears before lying down so they didn't have any more run-ins with the nixies. Without Tiger Lily trying to kill them, the journey out of the jungle was far less eventful than their journey into it had been. Still, there was that one moment with a large spider that gave her the shivers.

Although Kalen and Talen kept watch, as they neared the edge of the jungle, Rommy felt herself relaxing. They had all made it. With all the narrow escapes they had had, it seemed like a small miracle and a good omen for the quest that awaited them.

As they reached the end of the path at the jungle's edge and stepped out from beneath the vast canopy, the sun lay low on the horizon.

Everyone seemed relieved to have made it out of the jungle in one piece. Lobo stood at the edge of the cliff, looking out. She walked up beside him and put her hand on his massive shoulder.

"Thank you for leading us," she said. "We'd never have made it without you."

"You are a brave youngling," said Lobo, turning his head to look at her. "I am proud to have helped you find your way."

"Will you could come with us?" she asked, holding her breath.

Lobo shook his head and gave a soft whine. "No, I must go back to my pack. It's a long time to be away from them," he said. At Rommy's expression, he nuzzled her cheek. "That doesn't mean we won't travel together again."

Suddenly Lobo lifted his head, his ears pricking forward. He nudged Rommy back toward the jungle.

"What is it?" Rommy asked, tensing and looking past him.

"Someone is coming," Lobo said. "We must get into the shelter of the trees."

Rommy turned, waving her arms at the others. Suddenly, she was flat on her back, her head thumping onto the ground. All the air went out of her in a whoosh, and Lobo's big head filled her vision. All she could see was his mouth drawn into a snarl as she tried to suck air into her lungs.

He shuddered, pointed his nose toward the sky, and gave a long howl that made all the hair on Rommy's neck stand up.

Finn's shout and Alice's wail had her twisting her head to see what was happening, but the big black wolf wouldn't move. He simply stood over her, his front paws pinning her to the earth.

"Lobo," she gasped out, "let me up." The wolf didn't move or make a sound. In fact, he didn't seem to hear her at all. His eyes were staring and glassy.

A high crowing sound made her blood ran cold.

Pan had found them.

Then Lobo's back legs gave way, and he sank toward the ground. His front legs were quivering, and then she saw it. Two darts protruded from his side. He shook all over, but he kept his big body over hers, blocking her from the sky beyond the cliffs.

"No! Oh, Lobo, no!" she said, trying to push the wolf off so that she could help him.

He gave his head a shake, and his eyes focused on her. "You must stay safe," he said, panting. "You must stop the boy who never grows up but never grows wise."

There was the sound of branches cracking and twigs snapping, and then Lobo's pack was surrounding them, snarling, hackles raised.

Lobo sank onto his side, and Rommy pulled herself out from beneath the wolf. She lifted his big head into her lap as tears ran down her face. "You can't die, Lobo," she whispered. "I need you. We all need you. How will we find our way without you?"

The wolf's one visible blue eye met hers and then flickered shut. He licked her hand. "You...are...strong...youngling," he paused, his breathing labored. "You...already...know the...way."

The big wolf let out a long sigh and then was still.

"No!" Rommy cried, bending her head as her tears fell thick and fast.

Pan's mocking voice brought her head up, and she wiped at the tears on her face before gently laying Lobo's head on the ground. She stood to her feet and moved closer to the edge of the cliff.

"'Stay back,'" said Finn. He had dragged Alice back into the cover of the jungle and was struggling to hold onto her.

"Stay back," Pan mimicked Finn, looking into the jungle. "Oh, so concerned about our little Rommy, aren't you? You'll be sorry you left, traitor." He swiveled toward Rommy and pointed his finger at her. "You stole away one of my Lost Boys. Finn was loyal to me before you got here. You've ruined everything, and now I hear you want to seal me away on this island forever."

"I didn't steal anyone, Pan," Rommy said. "You're the one who's been stealing children. If you'd just stop..."

"They're better off with me," he said, both his hands curling into fists. "Adults are all worthless. The boys are happier here than stuck with a bunch of liars." He tilted his head, staring at her. "You'd be better off with me, too. What has your father done for you, anyway?"

"I've told you before, I'm not joining you," said Rommy, shaking her head. "I belong with my father, just like those boys belong with their parents."

"Ha! You don't know anything, but I'll make you see. You all see eventually," said Pan, frowning.

He stuck two fingers into his mouth and gave a piercing whistle. Two of the older Lost Boys—Rommy thought one of them was Oscar—came flying up with a struggling figure between them. Pan stuck a thumb out in the trio's direction and smiled again, all his teeth showing. "I thought she could help persuade you."

"You're nothing but a git full of tosh," a familiar voice shouted.

"Francie?" Rommy gasped.

Pan let out a maniacal laugh. "You took one of my Lost Boys, so turnabout is only fair play. After all, persuading children to come to Neverland is my specialty. You said so yourself."

"Rommy?" Francie shook back the black curls tangled around her face. "Who is this idiot boy, and what is going on?"

Pan flew in a lazy circle around Francie and the two Lost Boys. She tried to kick him, but he only laughed. "I like her! She'll make almost as good of a Lost Boy as Finn." He put his hand on his chin, his eyes sparkling with mischief. "Of course, she has to get used to the idea first."

"You are balmy on the crumpet, mister!" shouted Francie, still twisting and trying to pull away from the two Lost Boys. "If you think I'm going to stay with you, you've got mash for brains."

Pan wagged his finger at Francie, but he stayed well away from her flailing legs. Then he spun back toward Rommy. The smile was gone, and his face screwed up in a scowl. "If you'd just listen, nobody would have had to get hurt." He pointed a finger at her. "You killed the wolf."

Rommy leaped toward Pan, but a sharp tug stopped her. Artemis had clamped her teeth on the back of Rommy's shirt.

Bardolf paced toward the cliff's edge, his mouth pulling back in a growl. "Don't waste Lobo's sacrifice," he said to Rommy. He turned his great head toward Pan, and his lips pulled back into a snarl. His voice sounded low and rumbling. "You are the one who blew the poison darts, Pan. We will not forget this. Remember that the next time you enter this jungle."

Pan shrugged his shoulders and ignored the wolf leader, turning his attention back to Rommy. "You won't always have this wolf pack to protect you, Rommy, or your precious father. He's back, you know. Should I tell him where to find you? I'm not sure he wants to see you, though. He looked awfully angry, and you know how adults are when they're angry. He'll probably wipe his hands of you. Then you won't have a choice. You'll have to join me."

"My father won't abandon me, and I'm never joining you," said Rommy. A thought popped into her head. "Is that what happened to you? Did your father abandon you, Pan?"

Pan zipped to only yards from where Rommy stood on the cliff's edge, Artemis still holding onto her shirt. His eyes were wild, and when he spoke, spit flew from his mouth. "Shut up! You don't know anything about me!" He gestured at the two Lost Boys, who flew away with the struggling Francie.

"We'll come for you," yelled Rommy at her friend's retreating back.

"Don't count on it," said Pan, now smiling again. "You know where to find me. I'll be waiting for you, but don't take too long."

With a last crowing laugh, Pan whirled and was gone.

Rommy stared after him, disbelieving, and slowly sank to her knees.

Chapter 33:
Leader of the Pack

Wolves surrounded Rommy when Finn and Alice pushed their way to where she knelt, her hands over her face. She was too shocked even to cry. The enormity of what had happened crashed over her like a wave.

One part of her mind heard Alice sobbing, and she realized she should comfort the little girl. But a numbness kept her rooted in place.

Despite her body's paralysis, her mind whirred. How had Pan gotten Francie? More importantly, what was he going to do with her? She felt Alice nestle into her side. Her tears soaked through Rommy's shirt, and her arms automatically closed around the small girl.

They stayed that way for a long moment. When Rommy looked up, her eyes found Finn's. "Oh, Finn, what am I going to do? How will we save Francie and find the key and get to the door and...what about my father?" She put a hand back over her face. "And Lobo, poor Lobo. I can't believe he's dead." This time the tears pushed their way out. "He died...saving....me," she said, a sob breaking free.

An arm came around her shoulders, someone holding onto her. "It'll be all right," said Finn. "We'll figure it out." He gave a short laugh. "You always figure out a way, and you'll do it again."

Rommy shook her head and leaned into his strength. "Not this time," she said, her voice muffled in his shoulder.

She could feel Alice's arms hugging her back and the soft humming of the fairies. Eventually, her tears slowed. She sniffed and wiped at her eyes. She couldn't just fall apart. Francie needed her and so did Alice. And perhaps even Finn, too.

And the wolves. They had lost their pack member. Because of her.

Rommy gently set Alice away from her and let Finn help her to her feet. She wiped at her face again, squaring her shoulders.

She turned toward Bardolf and bowed her head in his direction. "I am sorry for the loss of your pack member," she said. "He was brave, and it was only because of him that we could complete our journey."

The big wolf stepped closer to her and acknowledged her words by touching his muzzle to the center of her chest. "Lobo was much fonder of humans than any of the rest of us, but he would not have volunteered if he did not see a bit of the wolf in you. Your sorrow over his passing does you credit." Artemis had stepped next to her mate and nuzzled his neck. "Pan will be sorry if he comes into our jungle, but you will always have safe passage here. We will honor Lobo's loyalty to you."

Rommy bowed her head once more. "Thank you," she said. She met the wolf leader's eyes, hazel to golden. An understanding passed between them. Then the moment was gone, and the wolf pack melted back into the forest. She looked back at Lobo's body still on the ground, wondering if they should try to bury him. While she watched, a silver mist covered Lobo's body. Then, a wisp of silvery smoke rose into the air. When the mist cleared, his body was gone.

Rommy turned, and found Finn, Alice, and the three fairies stared at her, waiting for what they should do next. She wasn't sure how she had become the leader of this ragtag group—a Lost boy, a homeless girl, and four fairies, one of whom was very grumpy—but she was. They were all looking to her to know what to do next.

Looking at their expectant faces, a heavy weight settled on Rommy's shoulders. "I think we should go see Little Owl," she said finally. "She'll want to know what's happened and will be worried. Plus, maybe she'll be able to tell us where we can start looking for Tinkerbell."

"What about your friend, Francie?" asked Finn.

"Francie can hold her own until we figure out how to get her away from Pan," said Rommy. She gave a grim smile. "Pan may have bitten off more than he can chew."

"How about your old man?" asked Alice. Her tears had stopped, but the little girl kept glancing to where Lobo had been lying. "Should we send a message or something? He's going to be awful sore we skipped out on him."

"Papa will have to wait," said Rommy. "I don't want him to worry, but he'll just try to stop me. And if I go back, I'll never get away again. He'll try to tuck me away somewhere safe." She looked at Finn, who had the grace to duck his head. "I can't let that happen until we find this key and turn that lock."

Rommy looked at the fairies. "You don't have to come with us, you know," she said. "You did more than your fair share in helping us find Unilisi."

Balo glowered at her. "Oh, so now that the hard part is over, you want to get rid of us," he grumbled. "Well, you can just take that thought right out of your head. If you think I'm going to just flutter off to please you, you have another thing coming."

A smile tugged at her lips, but Rommy managed to keep a straight face. Nissa alighted on Finn's shoulder. "We will help you, Andromeda Cavendish. We will help you with your quest."

Kalen and Talen lifted their tiny spears to show they were with her.

She looked at all of them. "Well, I guess we better get started," she said.

Together they pushed off the ground and into the air. With Rommy leading the way, they headed toward Little Owl's home. As they flew, Rommy wasn't sure how they would accomplish rescuing Francie, dealing with her father, and closing the passage to Neverland. But she had spent most of her time since she had left Chattingham's not knowing what she was doing. It hadn't stopped her yet.

Afterward

Thanks for picking up *Pan's Secret!* I hope you enjoyed it. If you have a minute, **I'd love it if you'd leave an honest review** on your online retailer of choice or Goodreads. This helps other people find the book, too.

If you'd like to keep up with my new releases, favorite book deals, and fun giveaways, be sure to sign up for my monthly newsletter. As a thank you for signing up, you will receive a free digital bookclub toolkit. You can sign up at http://www.rvbowman.com/u4fz.

If you want to check out the other books in the **Pirate Princess Chronicles**, you can get *Hook's Daughter (book 1)* **and** *Neverland's Key (book 3)*.

Don't miss out!

Visit the website below and you can sign up to receive emails whenever R.V. Bowman publishes a new book. There's no charge and no obligation.

https://books2read.com/r/B-A-JZDH-KJZBB

BOOKS 2 READ

Connecting independent readers to independent writers.

Did you love *Pan's Secret: A Pirate Princess's Quest for Answers*? Then you should read *Neverland's Key: A Pirate Princess's Last Chance*[1] by R.V. Bowman!

[2]

A crazy fairy, murderous mermaids, and a looming deadline - what could possibly go wrong?

Rommy knows what she has to do - stop Pan. She knows how to do it - find the key and turn it in the lock. She knows what's at stake if she fails - being stuck in Neverland forever.

What she doesn't know is how she'll accomplish it all *and* persuade her father to give up his desire for revenge before the sun comes up.

Join Rommy and her friends on their final quest where they will have to deal with poisonous swamp cats, learn how to breathe underwater, and overcome the biggest obstacle of all - their own failings.

If you like fast-paced fantasy adventures with pirates and spunky heroines set in fantastical worlds, you'll love *Neverland's Key: A Pirate Princess's Last Chance*, the final installment of the middle-grade fantasy-adventure trilogy the *Pirate Princess Chronicles*.

Pick up *Neverland's Key* and join the final adventure today! Read more at www.rvbowman.com.

About the Author

R.V. Bowman spends her days wrangling middle-school students while secretly trying to instill a love of language without any of them realizing it. By night, she writes fantastical adventures full of magic and heart.

Her love of books began as a child when she would pester anyone within earshot to read her a story. Once she learned to read on her own, her grandmother fed her reading addiction with a steady supply of books. R.V. Bowman lives in Northwest Ohio with her husband, two sons, and a very hairy dog named Kipper.

Read more at www.rvbowman.com.

Made in the USA
Middletown, DE
16 March 2021